Hunted
W

Devil Mountain Wolf Shifters: Book Eight

A Paranormal Menage Romance

Jasmine Wylder

© Copyright 2020 by Pure Passion Reads - All rights reserved.
1. Edition

Title: Hunted by the Wolves
ISBN: 9798656616249
Author: Jasmine Wylder
Publication Date: June 24, 2020
Publisher: Pure Passion Reads GmbH, Uferstr. 3a, 39307 Roßdorf

In no way is it legal to reproduce, duplicate, or transmit any part of this document in either electronic means or in printed format. Recording of this publication is strictly prohibited and any storage of this document is not allowed unless with written permission from the publisher. All rights reserved.

Respective publisher owns all copyrights not held by the author.

DEDICATION

To my loved ones B & B, who encouraged me to fly toward my dream:
Let's soar.

CONTENTS

Chapter One	8
Chapter Two	15
Chapter Three	22
Chapter Four	29
Chapter Five	36
Chapter Six	43
Chapter Seven	49
Chapter Eight	56
Chapter Nine	63
Chapter Ten	70
Chapter Eleven	77
Chapter Twelve	84
Chapter Thirteen	91
Chapter Fourteen	98
Chapter Fifteen	105
Chapter Sixteen	112
Chapter Seventeen	119
Chapter Eighteen	126

Chapter Nineteen	133
Epilogue	138
Thank You!	144
About the Author	145

CHAPTER ONE

Trevor lifted his sharp muzzle to the sky, inhaling deeply. There was a hint of rain in the forest, the leaves and ground slightly damp from the mist that had swept in at dusk. Now, at midnight, everything was still and silent. More silent than it had any right to be, but that only meant that the woodland creatures were burrowed away.

They were close to their quarry. It had taken them almost three weeks to track it down, but finally, they had found it. Here, in the midst of the deep uninhabited forest.

It was several months since they had heard about this hunting competition. Shifters all over the world were invited to participate. To find the prize and hold it against other shifters trying to take it. Everyone who signed up was given an implant in their arm to be checked on every few days to make sure they were still in the running. If they lost their implant, then they no longer could participate in the hunt.

While many of their competitors had decided the best way to win was to attack others and remove those implants, Trevor and Clinton had challenged themselves to find the prize. Technically, the location was supposed to be released in a few days, but nowhere in the rules did it say they had to wait until then to go retrieve their prize.

All they would have to do from there was hold the prize for four months, and then not only did they get to keep it, but they were also going to be given the million-dollar prize. The excitement for that money welled in Trevor as a distant light flashed between the trees. He crouched down, Clinton hunkering beside him. They both shifted back to their human forms.

"Alright, it looks like we're here," Clinton said. He grinned at his partner and Trevor's wolf growled lightly. It wanted to get a move-on already. After so much waiting and searching, they had the prize within their grasp. "You sure you don't want to hang back, wait until the others have thinned themselves out a little more before we snatch her?"

"I'm ready to get this prize." Trevor's gaze focused on the light. None of their pack mates had thought too highly of this. Hunting down a woman who would then be their mate, so Trevor and Clinton had told them it was about the money—and it was. It wasn't as though they had a signed contract saying that the prize had to stay with them to be their mate.

Trevor privately thought it would be a nice arrangement, even if it was him and Clinton being sugar daddies to a woman who liked the idea of being chased, but he hadn't said that. They needed to know what sort of woman the prize actually was.

They made their plan and shifted back to their wolf forms, breaking apart to come at the light from either direction. Trevor's whole body hummed with excitement; his ears perked up in mimicry of the wolf in his chest. It snarled lightly, full of energy that was burning to be released. His muscles bunched as he slinked through the woods.

Soon enough, he was only yards from a cabin. From inside, a warm glow pushed against the curtains hanging in the window. Trevor sniffed and paced around the outside, making sure to keep himself silent. There were no signs of any guards, no sign that she was being protected by anything besides those four walls.

Who knew what was inside, though? Trevor crouched down, peering around again as he looked for anything that might be a camera or a trap. It seemed as though she was completely unprotected, and he frowned. She would have been out here alone for several weeks already. To have no protection from the wild animals of this wood was poor planning on the committee's part. What was she supposed to do if a bear or cougar had wandered too close or decided that a human looked like a good snack?

Is she even human, though?

Nobody knew who the prize was or what she looked like, after all.

He'd know soon enough. Clinton gave a short bark from the other side of the cabin and they rushed it at the same time. Trevor shifted to human form, ramming himself against the door. It sprang open easily beneath his bulk. The light blazed and a woman screamed, but she was wearing one of those clay facemasks so he couldn't tell what she looked like. The cabin stunk of pomegranate lotion, a vaguely familiar scent.

Clinton climbed through the window in his wolf form.

"Clayton River competition?" Trevor asked, just to make sure that they didn't just barge in on some woman who had no part of this.

The woman nodded silently, her mouth gaping. Before she had a chance to speak, Trevor seized her and flung her over Clinton's back. She squealed and clung to his fur tightly as he bolted out the door. Trevor hung back, finding her backpack of clothing, and then followed them into the night.

It was dawn by the time the two of them stopped. In all this time, the woman hadn't said a word, just clinging to Clinton as they moved. When they got to the cave that they had previously decided to stop in, and where their clothes were, Clinton and Trevor shifted back to human form. They slapped each other on the back, laughing, and then turned to their prize.

The clay mask had dried, cracked, and flaked away. She wore baggy sweats and a sweater that wasn't quite enough to hide her curves. Her eyes were wide as she stared at the two of them. And Trevor's stomach swooped as he stared back into eyes that he knew all too well.

"Jessica Byrd?" he gasped, moving closer.

"Hi," Jessica breathed, her hands moving to twist in the hem of her sweater.

Clinton let out a string of curses that made her flinch. Trevor's wolf growled at him, but he ignored it as he continued to stare at Jessica. He scratched the back of his head, making a confused noise in his throat. What was she doing here? Had they been fed bad information?

"You are the prize for this competition?" Clinton demanded, turning back to them. His hands were clenched at his sides, his eyes narrowed. Looking far angrier than the situation called for, Trevor thought. But Clinton was a passionate guy, and he didn't like to be taken by surprise. He liked to be in control. "We should have known."

Trevor sighed as he turned to him. "How could we have known? The identity of the prize was never important, only finding out where she was so we could win the competition."

Here Jessica flinched, and Trevor turned back to her. His wolf nudged him in the ribs and this time he followed his instincts, moving to her side to put an arm around her shoulders. "Hey, it's okay. I know that this isn't what you expected, but everything is going to be okay. Sorry for jumping in there like we did. We were expecting more resistance."

"How did you even end up part of this?" Clinton snapped. "You told Beth that you weren't picked."

"Can you please get dressed?" Jessica blurted. She looked up at the ceiling of the cave. "This isn't a conversation I want to have while you're naked."

Trevor glanced down at himself. Yeah, Jessica would be bothered by their nudity. She was human and humans weren't as comfortable with the naked figure as shifters were. He grabbed his clothes and dressed. Clinton, grumbling, did the same. Once they were clothed, they turned back to her. She had taken a seat on a rolled-up sleeping bag, her legs tucked beneath her and her arms wrapped firmly around her middle.

"Well?" Clinton demanded, his eyes narrowed.

"Clint," Trevor murmured. "How about we not act like this is a personal affront to us, okay? It doesn't matter if the prize is Jessica. The plan's the same."

"Beth was giving me a hard time about signing up for the competition," Jessica said, twisting her hands. "She said that I was being reckless and that there were better ways to get men's attention. So I lied to her to get her off my back. I was selected as the prize and I… I just really wanted to… what are you doing here?" Her eyes narrowed as her hands clenched. "I thought Lucy was opposed to this."

Trevor flinched. Lucy, a wolf a few years older than himself and Clinton, had more or less raised them and their friends, William and Jacob, from the time they were in their early teens. She had been opposed to the whole idea of hunting down a woman to be their mate like some prized mare.

"Lucy knows we're here if that is what you are asking," Clinton said as he narrowed his eyes.

Trevor stepped in quickly to explain. "She doesn't like the idea of the prize woman being reduced to an object that can be kidnapped and passed around, but we explained that there was a thorough vetting in place to make sure that the woman wanted to be part of this. And you do want to be part of it, right?"

Jessica nodded.

"Well, there you go." Trevor gave her a smirk that had her blushing. "All of us are here because we want to be. So.

Just because we know each other doesn't change anything. We will still be holding onto you until it's time to take you to the drop zone, and then we'll be getting a million-dollar prize."

Jessica's shoulders slumped.

"It's better that you end up with us rather than some stranger, right?" Trevor pressed, not liking the look on her face. Like she had been defeated and lost something very important to her. "And I know that you'll be trying to get away from us because that's in the rules, but once this is done, we can take you back to Deville and—"

"I'm not going back to Deville," Jessica snapped. "There's nothing for me there. Working at the diner with customers who yell at me all the time? Being bored and lonely every night and every weekend? There's nothing to do there and there's nobody to do it with, not since Beth mated with William and Jacob. The girls in the book club have no time for me; they're all busy with their lives and families, and there is no way I'm ever going to have a family of my own if I stick around there!"

Clinton shrugged, still looking pissed off. "Then we won't take you back to Deville. Fine. You don't have to get so uptight about it."

Jessica leapt to her feet. "Don't you dare tell me what to feel! You don't know me. And no," she spat as she turned to Trevor, "it is *not* better that I know you. The point of this competition was for shifters to win me as a *mate*, not toss me over the finish line and laugh all the way to the bank!"

With a snort that didn't quite hide the guilt in his eyes, Clinton strode out of the cave. Trevor didn't bother trying to placate Jessica. He understood why she would be so upset. He would, too, if his plans had just come crumbling down. Her presence did mean things were going to get a little more complicated, but they could still work with it.

After Clinton was gone, Jessica slumped back to the floor and hid her face in her hands. "This was my last chance, and you've ruined everything."

"It's not your last chance," he told her softly. "And better us, who you know won't string you along, than someone who would lie to you about it, right?"

She looked up at him with an unconvinced glare.

"And you know that we plan to use that prize money wisely. We're going to add it to the college fund for the pack. And that's a worthy cause." Trevor crouched beside her. "Hey. Don't be so glum, Jessica. After all, we have four months. You could be kidnapped by a dozen other shifters by the time this is over."

He was met with a glare in response.

Trevor shrugged and stood. He walked to the mouth of the cave to stand guard. His wolf whined at him to go back to her, but he pushed it down. Yes. This had gotten a whole lot more complicated indeed.

CHAPTER TWO

A howl rang out somewhere in the distance and Jessica shivered. Was that a real wolf or was that a shifter? She wanted to ask, but one glance at Clinton's scowling face stopped her from doing that. He had returned shortly after he'd left, stating that they didn't have time to sit around moping. Jessica was surprised that they planned to continue on, but they didn't shift and let her ride again.

Instead, they pulled out the pack that she hadn't realized Trevor had packed and sifted through it until they found clothing that was more suited to walking through the forest than the sleepwear she had on. Once she had changed and put on her shoes, they looped a rope around her waist and tied one end to Trevor's belt and the other to Clinton's.

Then they started walking.

Jessica realized quickly what this was about. They were tiring her out so she couldn't run away from them. That was part of this competition, after all. She was meant to try to escape them. If she eluded the contestants and delivered herself to the finish line in four months, it would be her who won the million-dollar prize.

She hadn't expected that prospect to look so appealing. She had signed up for this thing because all her relationships had crashed and burned in the past. She was too fat for human guys to take a second look at her, and while shifters liked women on the curvier side, her attempts to find a mate through the Paranormal Marriage Agency had ended up in five disasters.

Trevor didn't understand that when she said this was her last chance, it really was her last chance. There was nothing else for her. No family, a burden to her friends, no prospects for any of the futures she wanted for herself. She wanted to get married. She wanted to have children. That was all she wanted. She'd thought about going to school, getting a career. She'd taken assessments, looked into various options. And it all left her feeling cold, with a dreadful feeling in the pit of her stomach. Like she was a failure for even looking at those options.

She lifted her hand to brush away a tear that had gathered on her lashes. "How did you find me, anyway?"

"We have our ways," Trevor said. He was following after her, helping her over fallen logs and the like. He gave her such a charming smile that she blushed, and that made her feel all the more miserable. If these two had any intention of taking a mate, she would have been a lot happier to see them.

"And how do you plan to keep me if other hunters show up?" she pressed.

"Beat them up and take out their implants," Clinton grunted ahead of them.

Jessica rolled her eyes, in part because of his attitude and in part because of his words. "You don't plan on killing them, do you?"

"Of course not," Trevor said with a frown. "That's against the rules."

Another howl, closer this time. Jessica swallowed hard, shivering. She hadn't anticipated this being as frightening as it was. Now that she was in this situation, she was almost embarrassed by the thoughts she'd had. A strapping, muscular shifter tracking her down at the cabin. Him opening the door, their eyes meeting and an instant connection blooming between the two of them. Running and hiding from the other competitors. Wild, delicious lovemaking in lakes, on beds of moss, against tress. Pretty much everywhere.

Sometimes she even imagined other competitors finding them in the midst of it and just watching. There was a secret thrill to the idea of being watched, no matter how much she wouldn't actually want someone to spy on her in real life.

Another howl, this time from their other side.

Trevor and Clinton both paused. They lifted their faces to the sky for a moment and then glanced at each other. Something silent passed between them, some sort of agreement, because they both acted without having to say anything.

They untied Jessica from their belts. She let out a surprised huff, but they then tied her ankles and wrists together. Jessica twisted her head away when they made to gag her.

"Don't you dare," she shrieked.

"We have to make sure you don't call out," Trevor explained. He held her head still while Clinton shoved a wad of fabric into her mouth and then wound a second strip of fabric around her head, tying it tightly over her mouth.

Jessica kicked the best she could, chewing angrily at the wad of fabric. It was dry and scratchy, sucking the moisture from her mouth as she tried to work it out through the narrow opening above the gag. It was all in vain, though. Trevor and Clinton stripped down—Jessica averted her eyes—and Clinton shifted to wolf form. Trevor slung her over his back and secured her.

All while butt naked.

Jessica closed her eyes, her cheeks warming at the proximity of his smooth, sculpted muscles. Tattoos played over his skin, and that brought up thoughts and memories she would rather not have at the moment. They weren't looking for a mate, after all. They were just going to use her and toss her aside.

Just like every other man in her life had done. Her father, every boyfriend she'd had, her ex-husband. If her mother were here, she'd tell her it was her own fault for being such a slut. After all, she was the one who'd had four boyfriends and two pregnancy scares by the time she was eighteen. It was because she'd slept with so many men before meeting her husband that he'd cheated on her—who wanted a used piece of gum like that, after all?

Tears burned against her eyes, but she blinked rapidly to get rid of them as they loped through the forest. Dawn was rising and the shadows were not quite so deep. She still had a chance here. Sure, Clinton and Trevor had her now, but that didn't mean that they'd keep her. And they would underestimate her because they thought they knew her.

If she wasn't going to get a mate out of this, the least she could do was get a million dollars. It would be enough to find something to do with her life. All the same, she hoped she would be able to find *someone*. There were a hundred contestants in this competition. There had to be at least one person who would be able to snatch her away from these two, the sexy wolves that she didn't have a chance for eternity with, and give her what she needed.

Jessica wiggled on Clinton's back, earning a growl from him, but she ignored the warning. She already knew that they weren't going to want to have anything to do with her, except for the prize money. They'd had their fun with her and said thanks and left. Sure it had been amazing, but she wasn't stupid. She recognized a one-night-stand when she had one.

She threw herself to one side, hoping that the ropes would loosen, but Trevor had tied her too well. She growled low in her throat as she struggled to free herself. The other howling was getting closer all the time, and now she was certain that there were other wolf shifters out there, on their track. Maybe one of them would actually want to keep her.

They had continued to run as dawn turned to morning. The howling faded slowly. Around noon, the wolves stopped and untied her, putting her on the ground. Both Trevor and Clinton were covered in sweat, and they only put on their boxers before pulling out a little food and water that they split between the three of them.

Jessica drank the water gratefully, her throat feeling scratchy from the gag.

"Were they watching you in that cabin?" Trevor asked as he crouched next to her.

Jessica shrugged, even though she knew that they had been. There had been a camera in the main room to keep an eye on her and make sure she was okay.

"They must have released her location early since we found her," Clinton growled. "It's not long until the first checkpoint, but we gotta get rid of that bear on our trail."

"Bear?" Jessica asked, blinking in surprise.

Neither of the wolves answered her. Instead, they quickly ushered her into a small group of trees and had her crouch down and once more tied her. Jessica sighed. She liked to be tied up in certain situations, but this was starting to feel excessive.

"My wrists are chafing," she complained.

Trevor took a moment to pull a couple pairs of silky underwear from her pack—she blushed again—and tuck them around her wrists beneath the ropes. She wanted to protest, but Clinton gagged her once more and they left her there, their supplies cushioned around her. At least Trevor had given her a pillow.

The sun was hot as it filtered through the trees, and Jessica laid there, annoyed—until there was a sudden yowling, howling, and roaring. Her heart leapt to her throat, and she jerked into a sitting position. Her hands were tied to a protruding root and so she remained half-hunched as the sounds reached her ears.

That didn't sound like a fight. It sounded like an all-out battle! Her heart thrummed in her chest, her eyes wide. A twig cracked and she jumped, turning painfully, to find herself staring into brilliantly green eyes. A black jaguar crouched nearby, its round face poking through the bushes to stare at her.

She screamed instinctively, the gag muffling the noise. She jerked back from the jaguar, yanking all the harder against her ropes. The jaguar lifted itself up—himself up, she saw—and winked at her. He was bigger than what a jaguar ought to be and it was that, and the wink, that made her realize that this wasn't some wild cat looking to rip her face off.

Her heart still pounded as she stopped struggling and waited. Would he untie her and take her away from Clinton and Trevor? Something tugged in her chest at that thought, but she pushed it aside. She waited, expecting the jaguar to do something. He sniffed at her, then sat, curling his tail around his feet as he studied her.

What was he waiting for?

Jessica squirmed. She bent over, managing to pull the gag from her mouth, and looked up again. "What are you doing?"

The jaguar gave a kitty-version of a smirk then turned and stalked away into the forest, leaving her where she was. Jessica blinked in surprise, her mouth slightly open. What was that about? Was he a guard for the competition or... or had he decided that she wasn't worth the effort?

It was only then that she realized that the sounds of the fighting had cut out. Moments later, the bushes rustled, and Trevor came into view. He was grinning, well pleased with himself, as he untied her and lifted her to her feet. The sight of the blood covering him made Jessica's stomach squeeze and her head feel light.

She opened her mouth, but all that came out was a little

squeak. Swallowing hard, she looked past him to see Clinton following after a giant man built like a brick wall. They were likewise covered in blood. Trevor pulled some bandages from one of his packs.

"And here she is," Trevor said, as he gestured for the other man to sit down. "The prize you are no longer eligible to have."

The man eyed her as he grunted. He sat and Trevor bandaged up his heavily-bleeding forearm. "If the two of you hadn't taken me by surprise…"

Clinton scowled where he was. "Well, we did. And we took out your implant so you're not part of the competition anymore."

Jessica sucked in a breath, fighting the urge to say something that would no doubt end with her being embarrassed. They'd taken down a bear? At least nobody had died… but, she thought as she looked at the muscles and tattoos this giant man had, it was a shame that he had lost. She could imagine spending the rest of her life with someone like that.

"All done," Trevor announced as he stood once more. "Now get your ass out of here."

The bear grunted and headed into the forest. Jessica stared after him, and Clinton growled at her. She jumped and was quiet as the two wolves returned her to her tied-up position on Clinton's back. She could tell them about the jaguar and his strange behavior—but if these two weren't going to keep her, maybe the jaguar would. So she remained silent.

CHAPTER THREE

They had to register having gotten Jessica at the first checkpoint. There were about a dozen of them peppered throughout the region, and they were only allowed to stay in them for a period of twenty-four hours. Trevor rolled his shoulders as they entered into the first checkpoint. Several other shifters were already in there, having gotten into a few fights from the state of them.

It was nothing more than a collection of tents, though, Trevor mused. He put an arm around Jessica's waist, smirking to himself as the other shifters took notice of them. Jessica ducked her head, blushing once more. It was surprising to him how much she did that. She looked rough, bits of that clay mask still coloring her face, streaks of sweat on her cheeks, her hair messy and pulled back into a bun that had been secured by a twig that Clinton had found.

"They're all jealous," Trevor whispered to her only to get a glare in return. He grinned at her and she rolled her eyes.

The competition runners, known by the bright blue vests they wore, exited the largest tent and came over to see them. Clinton and Trevor proudly presented Jessica, and the runners scanned their implants.

"First rights granted," one of them, a tall man whose voice vaguely resembled Morgan Freeman's, rumbled. "You are checked in for twenty-four hours. Replenish your supplies, get what treatment you need. Please enjoy your stay. The prize will be kept separate from you at this time, as she needs her rest as well. She will not be permitted to leave without you."

Trevor opened his mouth, about to protest. He didn't like the way the other shifters were eyeing her. His wolf stood up, fur on end as it growled fiercely. Clinton elbowed him in the ribs, though, and Trevor closed his mouth. This was part of the competition. The runners needed to be able to check Jessica over and ask her questions to make sure that she hadn't been mistreated in any way by the hunters.

Any mistreatment was an automatic disqualification. Which made Trevor wonder why they hadn't done a more thorough background check on them. It wasn't as though he and Clinton had anything bad in their past, but their complete disappearance from the world for six years when a dragon had taken them as slaves should have prompted at least some questions from the people organizing this.

All the same, Trevor was happy to be here. This wasn't just about the money. It was a chance for him and Clinton to prove themselves. To show that they still had the skills they developed in the few years they'd spent in the military.

After Jessica was led away, Clinton slapped Trevor's arm and jerked his chin toward an open area where there were several tables arranged and many shifters lounging about with drinks in their hands. Trevor grinned. Even though he hadn't been hurt badly in their fight with the bear, his muscles were tense from all the work he'd put them through, and he was interested in having a little bit of a relaxation time.

They got to a table, and Trevor reveled in the way people kept glancing at them. Awe in some faces, scowls on others, and still others cunning and watchful. The bear that they'd taken care of early was likewise there, drinking heavily. He ignored the two wolves, and Trevor was more than happy to ignore him right back.

A beer was put in front of him and he frowned up at the person who'd put it there. A man with green eyes and dark hair shorn close to his scalp on one side with the other side pulled into several braids smirked down at him.

"Well, it seems like the competition has kicked off to a good start," he said. "Congratulations. I didn't think that it would be a couple of wolves to find our prize first. I'm Nikola, by the way."

Clinton opened the beer Nikola handed him and snorted. "Thanks for your backhanded compliment, Nikola."

Trevor turned his frown to his partner. What was his problem? They didn't need to start antagonizing people here. They already had a target on their backs for bringing Jessica in before anybody else could. That right there earned them a nice little purse for the end of the competition. The last thing they needed was for these other shifters to start coming after them on a personal level, too.

Nikola, however, only smirked and walked away with a spring in his step. Trevor sniffed at his beer and tasted it, checking to see if it had been drugged somehow. Of course, that would be against the rules, but with a million-dollar prize on the line, he wasn't going to put it past anybody to break the rules to give themselves a head start.

There didn't seem to be anything wrong with the beer, though, so he drank it. It was cold and crisp running down his throat and his tense muscles unlocked. Now that they were here and they had Jessica, he and Clinton were going to be more careful moving forward. It wasn't a matter of making a mad dash now... from here on out, it was a matter of being smart.

A few of the other contestants tried to make small talk, but Clinton brushed them all off rather bluntly until Trevor pulled him to go check on Jessica. She was in a private tent with several guards around it, to make sure nobody tried to grab her. Clinton and Trevor, having registered her, were allowed in only after she granted them permission.

Which she didn't give. Not at once, at least. She came to the door of the tent and frowned at the two of them. "Come back in an hour or two, after I've had time to get some rest."

Clinton scowled, but Trevor tugged him away, nodding toward Jessica. "Have a good rest," he said brightly.

They went to their tent and crept in. There, they laid out their sleeping bags and rested their bodies. Trevor let out a sigh, about ready to fall asleep right then despite the light streaming from the afternoon sun. It was baking in the tent even though they were in a relatively shady place, but he stretched out, enjoying the warmth. His wolf made an annoyed sort of noise, wanting to go be with Jessica. It was ready to play. To turn her over in her sleeping bed and claim her loud enough for the whole camp to hear.

He smirked as he imagined it, one of his hands drifting down to massage himself through his pants. He hadn't really given it much thought, what they'd do in the four months keeping their prize out of the hands of other shifters, but seeing that it was Jessica? Well, he certainly had plans to keep himself from getting bored now…

A sharp smack on his wrist made him jump. He twisted to see Clinton scowling at him.

"What was that for?" Trevor demanded.

"You know exactly what it was for. Get your mind out of the gutter. We're in this for the money, not the woman. You need to remember that."

"You remember that," Trevor retorted childishly. He rolled his eyes and then rolled to his side, reaching into his pants this time. Clinton wasn't the boss of him. Besides which, Jessica was their prize. They had every right to claim her. There was nothing in the rules that said they couldn't fuck her.

And if any of the other contestants were looking for a mate rather than the money, claiming her would drive off a few of them at the very least.

***

Trevor didn't take long to find his completion, though his hand felt somewhat unsatisfactory when he remembered the smooth, lush body that belonged to Jessica. All her curves jiggling as he pounded in her or watched Clinton take her. She was a vocal one, and he longed to hear her crying out his name again. Sure things in Deville hadn't worked out so that they'd have a chance for a second go but out here? Well. He had every intention of having her again.

When they went back to her tent and she let them in, he told her that exactly. Her cheeks flushed dark red, her eyes widening in innocent surprise.

"What?" she blurted out.

"I said that the three of us could have a rematch," Trevor said, taking one of her hands in his. "It'd be fun, don't you think? The three of us fucking in here, all of them out there knowing exactly what we're doing and wishing they could fuck you, too."

Jessica covered her face with her hands. "Don't talk like that," she mumbled.

Trevor tugged her hands down and kissed her. His wolf growled in pleasure as she kissed back, moaning as her hands moved to grip his shirt. He hardened as he pressed her back until she was laying down. His hand started to seek out the bundle of nerves between her thighs when suddenly Clinton growled and yanked him back.

"Fucking hell!" Clinton breathed, glaring at the two of them. "What do you think you're doing?"

"Claiming my prize," Trevor snapped back at him. He kept his hands on Jessica, who was still red, still willing. The smell of her arousal was thick in the air. "She belongs to us, at least for the time being, so why shouldn't we?"

Clinton rolled his eyes. "You're a fucking idiot." Trevor

glared at him, but Clinton wasn't waiting for a rebuttal. "The other shifters are going to expect for us to stay here for the full twenty-four hours. We have to get out of here before they can set up ambushes. Didn't you notice that there were several of them gone already?"

Trevor hadn't noticed.

"Of course you didn't," Clinton snorted. "You were too busy imagining fucking Jessica. There will be time to fuck later, but right now we need to get on the move."

Jessica scooted back from them, her hands curling into her pants. She was wearing fresh clothes. "You're *not* going to tie me up again."

"We are," Clinton said as he pulled a length of rope from behind his back. "And we're leaving all our supplies here. The tent was watched; if we go back for them, they'll follow after us."

"But I…" Jessica's shoulders slumped. "Alright fine. But if you tie me up again, I am not going to let you fuck me."

Trevor's wolf growled. He understood what it was feeling—he had come in here ready to have some fun and Clinton had ruined it. Jessica had been very willing to have a little tango in the sheets, why did they have to leave now? Sure, they would likely exhaust themselves with sex if they started, but it wasn't like that was a bad thing. If they made the noise and everybody knew what was happening, it would drive some of their competition away and make even more of them think that they'd have until morning at the very least.

But Clinton had a point. They needed to get moving if they were going to get to their next stopping point. So he sighed, binding Jessica's wrists and gagging her once more. Clinton cut open the back of the tent and the three of them slipped out into the gathering dark of twilight.

They crept to the border zone of the checkpoint and shifted before heading into the woods once more. They traveled all night, not stopping when it started to rain. At one point, Trevor, scouting ahead, discovered a posse of lionesses, but they were able to circumvent the ambush.

Lionesses, he thought as the black of midnight wore to the light grey of dawn. *They must be after the money, too. Even if they were all lesbians or bisexual, they have each other; why would they want someone else?*

But they'd already passed them and didn't have to worry about them anymore. Dawn broke with Jessica nodding off on Clinton's back. Trevor was feeling pretty tired himself, his wolf unhappy with him for pushing so hard, but he popped a couple of caffeine pills and continued on.

It wasn't much farther before they reached their destination—a beautiful, wide, blue lake. The wolves shifted back to their human form and tugged Jessica down the narrow stream that fed into the lake.

"Where are we going?" she asked, her brow furrowed.

Trevor grinned at her as he looped her bound arms over his neck. "Straight down."

CHAPTER FOUR

Clinton shook the water free of his hair as he emerged into the little pocket of air that he and Trevor had built before this competition had started. Trevor and Jessica were already there, soaked to the bone but with the LED waterproof light that they had placed in their little pocket already on. It cast a bright, warm light that allowed Clinton to see just how much Jessica was shivering.

His wolf growled in his chest, pushing him toward Jessica, but he ignored it, instead turning to the supplies that they'd put here in their waterproof containers. His stomach growled, having had nothing since before they'd found Jessica at the cabin. He had noted how closely they were being watched at the checkpoint and hadn't eaten anything, to make the other contestants think that he planned to do so later.

"Let's get some heat on in here," Trevor said with a seductive grin at Jessica. She stared at him blankly, and Clinton rolled his eyes. He should have known that Trevor was going to end up thinking with his cock instead of his head. His partner never could keep it in his pants. Ever since they'd joined the wolf shifters of Devil Mountain, he'd been chasing everything in a skirt and pulling Clinton along for the ride.

Clinton had no problems with Trevor's taste. They always ended up fucking sexy women, each one more desirable than the last. They were all curves, all interesting and witty, all spitfires when they wanted to be and very into the whole kink scene that Clinton and Trevor liked. Jessica was no exception.

But the problem was the timing. Even though they were fairly certain that this little pocket was safe from detection, they couldn't be too careful.

"Here." Clinton handed Jessica a bottle of water. She fumbled with it and he cut through the wet ropes still holding her bound. When she gave him a surprised look, he shrugged. "You can't exactly run away here, can you? Get some water and we'll have food for you soon enough."

Jessica drank from the bottle and then looked at their little stove in alarm. "Won't that eat up all our oxygen?"

"No." Clinton pointed toward the ceiling, where several steel pipes peeked through the concrete they'd finagled here. "We built this place and we've got quite a few vents to the surface, to make sure we don't run out. There's also this." He pulled back two hanging sleeping bags to show a larger vent, which had grating over it to prevent unwelcome critters from finding their way inside. "This is our escape hatch. Big enough for us all to squiggle through in case we can't get out through the water."

Trevor smirked as he cut open a can of soup and set it to heat on top of the stove. "We know how to live underground, Jessica, and we'd never build a hideout that could suffocate us."

It was true. Clinton found himself relaxing despite himself. He hadn't been happy when he found out their prize was Jessica because he knew that it was going to cause complications. His wolf wanted her—bad. And he knew how Trevor would react—exactly as he did. But they couldn't afford the distraction. They had a mission. For the first time, they had the chance to really give back to the pack that had saved them from the gutter.

A chance to give back to Lucy. After all she had sacrificed and suffered through the years, the least they could do was give her the money she needed to get the university education she longed for. Or whatever else she wanted. They owed it to her, big time. His own parents had kicked him out. His siblings didn't want anything to do with him. Lucy not only took care of him and protected him, but she also taught him everything he knew. If it weren't for her, he'd have joined a gang and dragged Trevor into it with him. They'd both be dead in the streets by now if it weren't for Lucy.

He might not have been able to protect her in the past, but he was going to ensure that her future was a better one.

But here, within their little underground pocket, safe from prying eyes, the whining of his wolf was winning out. It wagged its tail as he moved a little closer to Jessica, enjoying her presence. Tears glinted at the corners of her eyes and he reached to touch one.

"Did you have someone in mind that you wanted to win this competition?" he asked, keeping his voice even.

Jessica shook her head. "I told you that I signed up hoping to finally get a mate."

"You can't have thought that it'd be some for-sure thing. That whoever first got you would be the person you were always destined to be with."

"So what if I did?" Jessica pulled back from him. "I'm allowed to have childish fantasies. I'm allowed to be disappointed that instead of being claimed by someone I have a chance to have an actual relationship with, I've ended up with a pair who have already fucked me and decided they didn't want me."

Clinton's brows rose. What was she talking about?

"Hey." Trevor moved around the stove and pointed at her. "I still want you, Jessica Byrd. If it were up to me, you'd be chained up to my bed back home, waiting for us to come back for you."

Clinton smacked his chest. That wasn't going to be helpful.

And he was right—but the damage was already done. Jessica dropped the water bottle. Her cheeks flushed dark and her hands clenched while her shoulders hunched in on themselves. She glared at the floor rather than Trevor.

"Right, because that is what I want to be," she spat. Her voice shook, but there was still a good load of venom in it. "To be a sex slave. Maybe that's what I should sign up for next. If I'm no good to have a proper relationship with, I might as well just spread my legs for whoever gives me a smile. Maybe I should start charging admission fees."

Clinton was surprised by the bitter words tumbling from her mouth. Jessica seemed to be surprised, too, because she pressed both her hands over her mouth, her eyes widening. As she glanced between them, she lowered her hands again and shook her head.

"No, I didn't mean that. I've thought several times I could be satisfied being just the… the friends-with-benefits girl. I like sex. I think I need sex more than I need romance. And I'm talking too much."

She turned away from them, still shivering in her wet clothes. Clinton stayed where he was. His wolf kept pawing and whimpering, but it was just as confused as he was. Where had this come from? How could a woman as sexy and beautiful and snappy as Jessica think that she was only good to be fucked and then left? And she was considering prostitution?

Anger welled in him, partly because he didn't understand how she could think sex work was all she was "good enough" for, partly because the thought of any other men drinking in her delicious curves made his blood boil. They wouldn't know how to treat her properly. Especially if they were human. He well understood why she wasn't interested in anybody in Deville—the available men were hardly the cream of the crop. More like men who couldn't be bothered to do enough thinking for themselves to want to change their lives by leaving the town. Those who did have drive, ambition, who were worthy of a woman like Jessica? Well, they weren't available. Married, partnered, or simply not interested in that sort of thing at all.

"Where is this coming from?" Trevor asked, crawling over to her. "Did you sleep with us because you thought we'd… you know. Make a commitment?"

Clinton flinched. He certainly hoped that wasn't the case!

Jessica hesitated a moment and shook her head. "No. I knew that you weren't interested in anything permanent."

"We're not," Clinton mumbled, checking the soup since there wasn't really anything else for him to do. "Trev and I decided long ago that we didn't want to have a mate. That we weren't going to have all the messiness that comes with love and romance."

Jessica flinched and he had to wonder how much of her words were true… and how much she had been hoping for this to end up as a fairy-tale ending. He scratched the back of his head while his wolf urged him to go to her, to prove that her words weren't right. That she was worth a lot more than just sex. But at the same time, the only thing he could think to do was to fuck her and how did that prove anything?

"You guys stopped coming to the diner," Jessica said softly. "Before, you would come to the diner all the time. And then you just… stopped… Like you couldn't even bear to look at me. What did I do wrong?"

She turned around even as Trevor reached to grip her shoulder. They both froze and Clinton bent over the soup, avoiding looking at either of them. This was not what he had thought this night would be. Sure, when he was planning out their victory he'd thought they would just hang out a few days here, until the other shifters had time to move on since they wouldn't think about a fucking pocket under the lake.

Since learning Jessica was their prize, he had been having certain fantasies not unlike Trevor's. They would have to be careful still since there was the possibility of people on the surface overhearing, but that was unlikely.

"You didn't do anything wrong," Trevor said slowly. He glanced back at Clinton, and Clinton returned the look with a slight shrug. He didn't know what they were supposed to do. "We just got busy. It's not like we stopped going to the diner for any reason."

Jessica didn't look convinced.

"You don't think we'd avoid you, do you?" Clinton asked. His tone was harsher than he wanted, but there wasn't really anything he could do about that, having already spoken. "We have no reason to avoid you. We had sex. It was fun. We weren't interested in anything long-term, but you said you weren't either."

Jessica flushed. "I'm not. Not with you two. You'll stay in Deville, and I don't want to stay there. There's nothing to do."

"Yeah, so what's the problem?" Clinton frowned at her, his wolf starting to get annoyed with him. It pushed him to go put her on her hands and knees so he could fuck her. The images kept floating in his mind and the conversation wasn't helping any. He wanted her. His wolf wanted her. He started to growl as Jessica stared at him, not answering.

Trevor smacked him across the chest, and he snarled at his partner, but Trevor only glared at him. "Growling isn't going to help anything."

"You already told her that you want to fuck her again, and she should know that if you're going to fuck her, I am too," Clinton answered. "So I don't get the point of this conversation. We didn't even know we'd stopped going to the diner," he added as he looked back to Jessica. "And considering that Trevor was ready to fuck you for the whole world to hear, you have no right to say we don't want you. So why don't you just take off those wet clothes and we'll show you just much we want to fuck you, huh?"

He said it challengingly. He didn't expect her to take him up on it. If anything, he expected her to fight back. He almost wanted her to fight back—but when she looked him in the eye, her gaze hardening, he did as well. Even before she stripped off her soaking shirt, he knew exactly what he wanted to do with her.

And as soon as her creamy skin was exposed to him, his wolf won the battle and he launched himself at her, eager to taste her pleasure again.

CHAPTER FIVE

Jessica wasn't really certain how their conversation had brought them to this point, but she didn't really care. The chill in her body was too deep to bear, and she needed the warmth of another person to banish the cold. It was more than just what was in her flesh; there was a dull, cold ache in her very soul, and she didn't know how to deal with it other than to throw herself into sex.

And so that was exactly what she did. Both Clinton and Trevor were all over her, their mouths hot and their hands hungry, before she had a chance to fully undress. After the chill from getting soaking wet, the warmth of them pressing in on her from either side was a welcome relief. Part of her wondered if this was a good idea since there was no possibility of this moving forward after the competition was over, but she decided she just didn't care.

Maybe forever wasn't possible for her. Maybe it was something that was a fairy tale or a dream. Why shouldn't she have what she wanted right here and now? If she couldn't have the family she wanted to create, why not just have glorious sex while she could?

"Do you want what we did last time?" Trevor asked her, kneeling to tug her pants down. Clinton lifted her slightly so Trevor could strip off her socks and shoes.

"But we don't have condoms and the lube for anal," Jessica said. She wrapped an arm around Clinton's neck while digging her other hand into Trevor's hair. It was still damp, although the little stove was warming the pocket quickly. "So we can't do that, can we?"

Clinton kissed her collarbone, his hands kneading her breasts. "There are other things we can do."

"But we can use—" Trevor started.

Clinton gave him a fierce glare that had a tingle running down Jessica's spine. They were so strong. So dominant. They could fuck her raw and painful and she wouldn't tell them no—it was just in the aura they gave off. Her mouth dried, and she wanted to tell Trevor to continue his suggestion, but Clinton's glare stopped her from speaking. Tingles ran through her body, craving their mouths on her once more and at the same time wanting to run.

How had she managed to find herself in this situation again?

"We are not fucking her ass without lube," Clinton snapped at Trevor. "I, for one, have no desire to tear her up and leave her trailing blood behind us."

"It doesn't have to be like that," Trevor groused back but didn't make whatever suggestion he had been thinking of.

Instead, he lifted one of her legs over his shoulder and buried his face into her. Jessica gasped as her clit throbbed. Her breasts felt like they were swelling beneath Clinton's touch and she clung to the both of them, her eyes wide as Trevor's tongue swiped and danced expertly. His eyes were turned upward, staring at her, while Clinton held her in place, hands pressed behind her with her elbows pinned to her sides.

"Once Trevor's done with you," Clinton breathed on her neck, his nose grazing her skin and causing shivers to shoot straight to her core, "I'm going to put you on your knees and put my cock in your mouth and choke you with it."

Jessica's lips parted, but the only noise she could make was a moan of pleasure. She nodded, agreeing to whatever Clinton wanted. She tried to break his grasp around her, but he only held tighter. Then a sharp whistle made Jessica jump and Trevor pull back. Jessica thrust her hips forward, whining in dismay at the loss of friction, but Clinton grabbed her hip and held her in place.

"Before we start getting really into this, we have to go over boundaries again," he growled, sounding angry.

Jessica flinched.

"Hey," Trevor murmured as he gripped her hips with his hands. "Why do you look guilty all of a sudden?"

Jessica chewed her lip and looked away. "I don't want to."

Trevor released her and started to move back, and she broke one arm free of Clinton, grabbing Trevor and holding him close. "No! I mean I don't want to go over boundaries. I don't want to think because if I start thinking, I'll end up overthinking, and then I'll hate myself because the reason I can't find someone who wants to keep me is because I'm an oversexed slut who watches too much porn and—"

She cut herself off as she pulled back from both of them. Tears blurred her vision as she looked around for her clothes. So much for not overthinking. What was she thinking? If the next shifters who grabbed her smelled them all over her, they weren't going to want to keep her, either. And sure, it might be fun to be kidnapped and fucked by a new man or group every few days (as exhausting as that would be), but she didn't sign up for this for random fucking.

She signed up for forever.

Not that I deserve it.

"Jessica," Clinton's voice was firm but gentle. "We set boundaries because we don't want to hurt you."

She gave up the search for her clothes. She had no idea how she'd lost them in this little area, but it didn't really matter. "Maybe I *want* you to hurt me! Maybe that's the reason why I'm still alone. Because I want you to do disgusting things to me, and I don't want you to hold back. Maybe it's because the ways I want to be treated mean that no decent man is ever going to—"

She cut herself off once more as Clinton and Trevor came at her. Her lungs froze up and she lifted both her hands, as though to ward them off.

Clinton took her hand and lead her to the stove, where the can of soup was bubbling, and Trevor wrapped a blanket around her shoulders. She saw several waterproof containers to one side, which had various clothing and supplies in them. No wonder they had been okay with leaving their stuff back at the checkpoint.

"Listen," Clinton said gently as he moved the soup off the stove and served it in three equal portions in camping mugs, "there is nothing wrong with wanting whatever it is you want. I know that human society likes to limit sexuality and honestly, that is a recipe for creating more weird stuff than just saying that everything goes so long as everyone is of age and giving full, willing consent. If you want to explore without boundaries, that is fine."

Jessica stared into her mug, the warmth seeping into her fingers. It did not feel as pleasant as the wolves' hands on her body, though.

"Also," Trevor said slowly, a pinch to his brow, "you have to remember that Clinton and I were held as slaves by that dragon for six years. We didn't have a lot of chances to explore our own sexuality and what was normal and not normal before we ended up having no outlets for our sexual desires. So, really… we're the last people to judge you for your kinks."

Kinks. Jessica sipped at her soup. Even though it had been bubbling on the stove, it was still rather tepid. She had never really considered what she wanted as 'kinks'. More like 'shameful desires that meant something was wrong with her and needed to be suppressed'. A long sigh fell from her lips as she shook her head.

"I want to," she murmured. "I just… don't think I should want to. But…" She looked up at them, flushing with embarrassment but unable to stop from blurting it out, "the thing is, I don't think I have boundaries at all. I want to be used like a ragdoll. I want to be beaten up and bruised and called horrible things. I want to be overpowered. I want to put up boundaries just for them to be ignored. I don't want a safe word. I want to… to… I don't want to be raped," she said, looking away again as her cheeks grew hot. "But I think I'd like to pretend that I am."

She didn't dare look at either of them. Her heart hammered in her chest as she tried not to imagine what their faces would look like now. Disgusted. Turned off. Maybe even a little hateful. Sure, Clinton had said he was going to choke her on his cock, and they had gotten a little rough when they had had their one-night stand but this… this was something else altogether.

"That…" Trevor said, his voice soft. "That is too extreme for me. At least right now. We don't have the relationship and trust that we need in order to explore something like that."

"Major turn-off," Clinton said. His voice was a little harder, but there still was no judgment in it. When Jessica finally peeked up through her lashes, she was shocked to see there was a contemplative look on his face. "But… but it's something that you shouldn't be ashamed of, either. It's tricky. For me, I'm afraid that I have been influenced too much by porn and will cross into that territory accidentally and really hurt my partners. I suppose, though, if everyone is in a safe setting where they feel comfortable and relaxed and can communicate beforehand what expectations are…"

Jessica's brow furrowed. Her own fantasies did disturb her deeply at times. But what Clinton was saying was to have someone that you already trusted… "You mean, like building up to it?"

"Yeah. And not having the fantasy every time. Gentle mixed with rough. That sort of thing."

The tension drained from Jessica's shoulders as Trevor nodded in agreement. She almost wasn't sure what to make of this. She hardly knew these two and yet they were making her feel so safe and secure in her own fantasies, the ones she had been ashamed of for so long. They were more than taking her seriously, they were helping her figure out a way she could stay safe and still indulge in that fantasy.

A pang hit her stomach as she reminded herself that this wasn't a forever situation. Neither of them was interested in building a relationship, even though they did say they'd wanted to fuck her again. Fucking was a lot different from a proper relationship.

A frown crossed her face. *But haven't I thought in the past I'd be happy being passed around and getting fucked by random men who were emotionally devoted to women who just couldn't keep up with them sexually?*

Jessica shook her head, sighing again. Was this just what she thought she wanted vs what she really wanted vs her overly ambitious sex drive coming into play?

"I'd still like to choke you with my cock," Clinton said casually. When she blushed, he sent her a wicked grin. "If you'd like to get back into that."

Jessica considered herself. Yes, there were lingering desires and being naked like this certainly opened everything up for the possibility of more… but at the same time, she was still confused. Her emotions were all over the place. And she was very tired. So she shook her head. "Not right now. Maybe after we've all had a chance to sleep and I have my head screwed back on straight."

Clinton and Trevor both looked disappointed, but they nodded their understanding. Trevor put on another can of soup as the first one had not been enough for three people. Jessica considered them silently as her mind turned over their conversation again and again.

The only problem was, she wasn't at all certain how she was supposed to think about any of this, let alone how she actually *felt*.

CHAPTER SIX

Jessica slept lightly in the pocket beneath the lake. Her brain didn't want to shut up, but the dreams that came with said light sleeping were pleasant to say the least. She wasn't in such a deep sleep that she wasn't aware that she was sleeping, and since she was aware they were dreams, she was able to change what was happening quite a bit. The dreams involved Trevor and Clinton—and all of them were naked.

She woke herself fully with a long moan. Her core was tight, aroused by the images in her dream. Another moan, this one of disappointment, rasped against her throat as she opened her eyes.

Trevor and Clinton were both awake. Both staring at her. Both with bulges in their boxers. Their shirts and pants lay tucked into the waterproof bag. They both stared at her lustily, even though Clinton coughed and turned his head away soon enough. Jessica realized that the blanket she was rolled in had wormed its way down her body, almost exposing her to view.

Feeling brazen (not to mention the heat that was burning in her from her unfulfilled start before she slept coupled with the dreams) she flipped the blanket all the way off.

Propping herself on her elbows, she gave the two wolves a little smile.

"Do you want to pick up where we left off? You never did choke me with your cock."

Clinton stripped off his boxers. He was already hard and ready. His fingers grazed against her lips, making them spark with desire, before moving to gently brush against her neck and down to her breasts. With a groan, he lowered his head, kissing one and then the other. Behind him, Trevor was lazier in taking off his clothes, folding them to one side with a smirk on his face saying he was enjoying the show.

Fire swept through Jessica as she gazed at first one and then the other, neither of them static, both in motion. It was almost impossible to believe that she was here with them. That once more they were looking at her with that burning lust that made tingles rush through her body. Her core ached to be filled with them once more.

Clinton grabbed her hip, flipping her up so he could press fully against her while giving Trevor room to sidle in from the back. Their warm bodies and hard cocks pressed against her, making moisture pool in her core. Thrills of excitement ran through her.

"Now," Clinton said, his hands all over her, joined now by Trevor's. "Before we get too carried away, we *have* to decide what we are going to do. There will be no anal because it's too risky without the lube, but was there anything else?"

"I don't mind trying it without—" Jessica started.

Clinton shook his head. "*No.* You have to respect our boundaries, too, Jessica. We might like it rough, but we don't want to actually hurt you. Not to mention it won't feel good for us, either. We'll stick with the sex that won't cause any real damage to any of us.

Jessica sighed, but she understood his point. It would be a difficult thing to explain away once they were at the next checkpoint, after all.

The thought that they didn't want to really hurt her, though, seemed... strange. Not that Clinton and Trevor were the kind to crave hurting other people. Quite the opposite from what Jessica saw. But somehow in her mind, she had always thought that dominating sex had to include some sort of pain to the submissive partner. And they were a dominant pair.

"We already decided that Jessica is going to give you oral," Trevor said, nodding to Clinton. "Or rather, that you're going to face-fuck her."

Jessica giggled, flushing. She nodded, eager to have his throbbing cock in her mouth, pushing so far in that she gagged. She curled one hand into Clinton's hair as he thrust his tongue into her mouth, a promise of what was to come. They didn't talk long before they'd decided what exactly they would try. Both of them were leery of tying her up this time, but they agreed to some other things.

The tattoos on both of their bodies rippled in the dim light. The stove had been put out quite a while ago, but with it being such a small space, it hadn't cooled down much despite the freezing water pressing in on them.

"You know what?" Clinton said as he put her on her hands and knees, while Trevor laid on his back, his face between her thighs. "I love how confident you are, Jessica. You have no hesitations with throwing yourself into sex, and that is such a fucking turn-on."

Jessica smiled in return, her whole body tense with desire. She never did understand why people felt the need to hide their bodies while engaging in these sorts of things. If they wanted to have sex with you, then they wanted to have sex with you. Anybody with eyes could see that she was no stick figure. If they wanted sex that meant they wanted to see her naked.

Still, she was nervous about Trevor's position. What if she crushed his face? But as Clinton and Trevor manipulated her position until she was in the one they wanted, those worries faded away. These wolves knew what they were doing, and if this didn't work they'd just find another position. Trevor's hands gripped her ass, pulling her apart so his tongue could work its wicked ways on her clit once more. She shuddered but barely had time to enjoy it before Clinton fisted her hair in his hand.

His grip was tight, a slight sting in her scalp. Jessica moaned, wanting him to really yank hard, but he was right… they weren't there yet. When he cradled her head between his hands, she opened her mouth obligingly. Clinton set a pace to begin with that was gentle, maybe a little too gentle. Her core twisted and tightened, tremors starting in her thighs as Trevor's grip tightened on her.

"Ready?" Clinton growled, stealing her gaze back to him. She hardly was able to nod with the way he was holding her, but somehow managed.

Clinton pushed in, deeper and deeper. When she gagged he paused—then thrust, reaching that depth while she choked on him. She loved every second of it and loved the look of determination and concentration on his face as he held her, stopping her from the instinctual pulling back her body wanted. Trevor caught her hands, holding them in place. Together, they overrode her body's instincts, just as she wanted them to.

"Put her on her back," Trevor said when she was seconds from climaxing.

Jessica gasped, half disappointed that they'd stopped, half relieved to have a reprieve. She didn't fight them or ask them what was happening next, although she had lost track of what the plan was. She smiled up at the two of them, her jaw aching slightly. They looked down at her with twin looks of lust and bent over her once more. Trevor gave her another few licks before he knelt over her torso.

Clinton was inside and fucking her wildly before she knew it. The pleasure swept through her so powerfully that she was left gasping and crying out, her hands immediately reaching for Trevor's knees. He laughed as her fingers dug into his skin, his own hands kneading her breasts. He plumped them together and slid his cock between them. His movements were lazy in comparison to Clinton and the contrast drove her crazy.

She didn't hold back in her vocalizations. She gasped, cried, shouted. At one point she started bucking her body, but the wolves took it as too similar to struggling to escape and so she made herself stay still. It was even harder than if she really had been trying to throw them off. Pleasure and desire burned through her. She never wanted this moment to end, didn't want to go back to the competition, didn't want to go back to her lonely, dreary life.

When she screamed, clamping down on Clinton. He fell forward with a series of grunts. Trevor laughed as he braced his partner. Clinton nipped at his shoulder and Trevor slipped out of the way, letting him fall to Jessica's mouth. His kisses were intense, passionate, as he continued to pound into her. Jessica returned the fervor in kind. They were like two people possessed, and they didn't stop until they were both utterly spent.

It was only after they were done that Jessica realized that they had left Trevor to take care of himself. He was wiping up, a pleased smile on his face. Jessica flushed slightly.

"Sorry," she croaked.

Trevor rose a brow. "What for?"

"You didn't get a proper turn."

Trevor laughed throatily and kissed her while Clinton still lay over her and inside of her. He was panting, his skin suctioned to hers with their sweat. Trevor traced a pattern on Jessica's hand, still laying lightly on Clinton's back.

"I'll have the next turn," he said with a wink. "But I think you need a little rest before we get to that."

"No, I don't," Jessica replied at once. Her whole body ached, but she hadn't reached breaking point yet. "I won't be able to relax until you've finished in me, too. Please, Trevor."

Clinton eased himself out and rolled off of her. He

laughed breathlessly. "Go for it, Trev. Who are we to deny the lady her demands?"

Trevor grinned as he launched himself onto her. Jessica welcomed the embrace, exhausted already but pushing herself to match Trevor. To embrace the burn of skin on skin, the heat created by the friction between them.

CHAPTER SEVEN

Clinton's wolf woke him, growling and nudging him in the ribs. He swatted at it, not wanting to wake from the warm, comfortable feeling of Jessica pressed against his back, blankets slung over the both of them and Trevor. But his wolf snarled, all but yelling at him to get up. With a scowl, he slowly pulled himself toward the day. They were a little behind schedule, but that was okay. It just gave the other shifters more time to assume they'd left the area, which would allow them more space to get to their next hideout.
He rolled slightly toward Jessica. Maybe they'd have time for a little more fun… although, he had to admit that they should hold off on that. Make sure that she could travel. When he pressed back against her more firmly, though, he was surprised that she wasn't as soft as she ought to be.
Lifting his head, he twisted to find that Jessica wasn't between him and Trevor at all. He was leaning right against his partner, and Jessica was nowhere to be seen. It wasn't just that she wasn't in the blankets anymore—she wasn't in the little pocket.
Clinton jumped to his feet, cursing loudly. Trevor jerked awake, letting out a sharp yelp as he did so. He bolted up,

hands balled into fists and ready to fight as he blinked around blearily.

"Jessica's gone," Clinton snarled at him. He grabbed one of the waterproof bags and began shoving stuff back into it. "She must have slipped out while we were sleeping. What was she thinking? She could drown!"

Trevor didn't respond. Wide awake now, he nodded at Clinton once and dove for the entrance. Clinton let him go. It was impossible to tell how far ahead of them Jessica was—or if she had gotten stuck beneath the lake's surface. His wolf growled, pacing, but Clinton forced himself to finish packing up their stuff. He dragged it all to the surface, slapping it onto the beach where Trevor waited, still naked.

"She left prints," Trevor called over his shoulder.

Relief washed over Clinton. "So she made it out."

Trevor nodded and stood. His expression was grim. "And she ran straight into those lionesses that had been hanging around. Their tracks are all together. We lost our prize, Clinton."

Another bout of swearing burst from Clinton. His hands curled into fists and his wolf growled loud enough to make his hair stand on end. He turned to Trevor, about to tell him that they would just have to reclaim their prize, but as he did so, a dark shadow slinking in the trees caught his eye.

A howl burst from him as he shifted forms, letting his clothing shred. He left Trevor and the supplies behind as he tore at the black jaguar. It hissed, ears pressing against its skull, before it sprang into the air. Clinton jumped after it, his teeth nearly catching the cat's tail. The jaguar leapt from tree to tree, Clinton chasing after it. They already had a pack of lionesses to deal with; the last thing they needed was another cat hanging around to snatch Jessica once they got her back!

Trevor howling made Clinton pause in his chase. The jaguar slowed, looked back, and then hissed again. It loped to the ground and padded away, as though completely assured that Clinton wouldn't chase it anymore.

He hated that it was right.

Grumbling to himself and his wolf growling, Clinton turned back around. He trotted back through the forest, following Trevor's calls until he got to where his partner was. He'd left the lake, winding his way into the forest. Upon seeing him, Trevor shifted back to human form.

Behind him, a good half-dozen women wearing absolutely nothing were packing up a camp. They all looked ticked off and glared at him. Clinton noted that every one of them had bandages on their forearms. Their implants had been taken out, then?

Clinton shifted back to human form. "What is going on here? You didn't get them all did you?"

Trevor looked grim as he shook his head.

One of the lionesses trotted over to him. She glared at him with amber eyes as she poked him in the chest. "No wolf would stand a chance against us. We were set on by a dragon. Fuck this shit. We sign up as a protest to the sexism inherent in this contest and as soon as we get the girl, she's snatched away from us."

Clinton tensed. "A dragon?"

"Only four dragons were allowed to enter," Trevor said grimly. "Because they'd have an unfair advantage."

Clinton fought against the renewed snarling of his wolf. He wanted to hunt this dragon down and kill it before it had a chance to lay a finger on Jessica—but there were the competition rules to be aware of, not to mention that killing a competitor was the fastest way to land in jail. Also, just because it was a dragon didn't mean that it was the same kind of dragon that took him, Trevor, and the others as slaves...

The tension clenching his jaw would not loosen, though. No matter how hard he tried to relax his body. Tremors shook his hands. They would deal with the dragon. For now, there was something else that he had to figure out before it became an issue again. "How did you know where to find us?"

The lioness looked him up and down. "Didn't you hear me when I said we joined up in protest against the competition? What makes you think that we're going to help you now? We got the girl away from you for a reason."

"Her name is Jessica," Clinton snapped. "If you cared about her and her choices then you'd have at the very least asked her name when you found her on the beach."

The lioness flinched but threw back her hair and put her hands on her hips. "Oh, so you're going to pretend like you care about her, are you?"

Clinton growled, his hands curling into fists.

Trevor grabbed his arm and pulled him back. "We don't plan on taking her as a mate if that's what you're saying," he said smoothly. "But we know each other. Jessica has been living the past few years in the same town as us. And she was very eager to sign up for this competition. It's through her that we learned about it."

"And if you don't want her, then what do you want?" the lioness scoffed.

"The prize money. We didn't know that it was Jessica who had been selected as the prize," Trevor said slowly. "But even if it were someone else, we wouldn't want her to be frightened. Which she must be right now."

Clinton was uncomfortably reminded that Jessica did want a mate out of this. Although why she thought that this was the best way to get someone who wanted her as a mate—her, Jessica Byrd, not just some random warm body that didn't mean anything—Clinton didn't know. She was really selling herself short, he thought.

And remembering her admission to that fantasy of hers… It made his frown deepen. A woman like Jessica shouldn't think she deserved that treatment—no person should. He wasn't entirely certain what to make of it. Was it just fantasy for her or was there a deeper issue that was causing her to desire such things?

He shook those thoughts from his head. He firmly believed that if the people involved in kink and fantasy were fully aware, willing, and of age, without any of the participants being manipulated or groomed in any way, then all was fair, so long as it stayed safe and consensual. Gods knew he had some disturbing fantasies, too. Not anything that went as far as wanting to play at rape, but if he was honest, he didn't know what was normal in human sexuality and what wasn't—or what was normal for him.

Or if he could ever have anything that could be remotely considered 'normal'.

"If it helps," Trevor was saying, and Clinton forced himself to pay attention again. "Jessica signed up wanting to be a participant. She wasn't thrilled about the two of us finding her because she wants a proper mate but…" He shrugged as a slight smile tugged at his lips. "We're not about to let anybody hurt her."

The lioness narrowed her eyes at him. "Really? And is that why she smelled like sex when we picked her up?"

"We had a sexual relationship before and Jessica wanted to have it again," Trevor said with a shrug. "It was fun; the three of us had a good time. And we made sure that we all had boundaries in place, so what's the harm?"

Clinton's wolf growled and tugged on his ribs, making him turn. They weren't going to get any help from the lionesses, and it didn't matter. They were wasting valuable time while Jessica was in the hands of a dragon! Where to start, though? His mind flashed to the jaguar—maybe it would know something. But he dismissed the thought soon enough. If it did, why would it be stalking him and Trevor, instead of going after the dragon and Jessica?

"Come on, Trevor," he said over his shoulder. "Let's find where that dragon took Jessica already."

He stalked back toward the lake, where their supplies had been left. Trevor caught up with him soon enough, but before they had a chance to shift back into their wolf forms, a small lioness, younger than the others, had stepped out of the bushes. She wrung her hands, looking nervous as she glanced back at the camp.

"Jessica protested when we picked her up, and that's the only reason I'm telling you this," the lioness murmured. "She wasn't taken by a dragon at all."

Clinton's brows rose.

"We were attacked by a dragon, but I gave Jessica the keys to my car and told her where to find it. She took off while the dragon was busy removing our implants. If the dragon hasn't found her, she'll probably be getting to the car now. It was about five miles east of here. If you move quickly you might be able to find her."

Clinton ground his teeth together as he nodded. He didn't like this idea. While it was better than Jessica not be in the hands of a dragon, at the same time she was out in the woods by herself. Any of the other competitors could find her and then what? Not to mention what might happen if she got lost!

He and Trevor were off again soon enough, leaving the lionesses behind.

They stopped by the lake to get their things—there was no use in picking up Jessica's trail if they were going to starve themselves after all—and headed in the direction the little lioness had told them to go. They picked up Jessica's trail quickly enough and Clinton pushed himself and Trevor hard to follow it.

They arrived at the car just as Jessica was getting into it. Clinton put on a burst of speed as the engine turned over. He shifted, leaping up to land on the hood of the car. Jessica let out a shriek. She clutched at her chest as she sat there staring at him.

"Unlock the doors," Trevor ordered her from the passenger side.

Jessica did as she was told, and Trevor slid in and took the keys.

"How did you two find me?" Jessica demanded.

"By following you," Clinton replied. He jumped off the car. "Let's get our stuff in the trunk and then head out. We weren't planning on a car, but it will be a help anyway."

Jessica let out a little snort. She was still soaked through, so Clinton dug in one of the bags for fresh clothing that she could change into on the drive. She took them without a word and soon enough, they were driving through the trees.

Just before they turned onto the highway, Clinton caught sight of a black jaguar perched in a tree, tail flicking and mouth open in what appeared to be laughter.

CHAPTER EIGHT

Trevor stood at the window, gazing out into the dark and watching for any sign of that fucking black jaguar. He'd been stalking them for almost a week now, always seeming to know where they were. He hadn't tried to confront them at all, but neither of the wolves liked to have him around all the same. They knew how dangerous it was to be watched, after all.

Jessica lay in a sleeping bag on the floor, Clinton stretched out beside her. They had only gotten to this old cabin in the last half-hour, and despite what a quick pace they'd set for traveling, none of them were notably tired yet. Trevor had volunteered to take first watch, but Jessica was very tense in her sleeping bag.

Eventually, she let out a huff and wiggled further away from Clinton. "Give me some space," she snapped.

Clinton rolled his eyes and went to lay across the doorstep instead. With Trevor at the only window, there was no way Jessica was sneaking away from them again.

"How did you find all these places anyway?" Jessica asked, as though the darkness weighed too heavily on her. They didn't allow any sort of light and it was clear that she wasn't comfortable.

"We heard about it from the other wolf shifters of Devil Mountain," Trevor replied, continuing to look outside. Clinton would have remained silent, not answering her questions. "This is an old safehouse that the Blaze Ops used to use."

"Blaze Ops?"

Trevor hummed. "They're a team of dragons that do off-the-record missions, although it's off-the-record that they do any sort of off-the-record missions. They operate out of the Magnus Academy and apparently they're pretty good guys." Here, Trevor shook his head. Only Sly, their alpha, and his second-in-command Devon did much with the Blaze Ops, but apparently, at one point, all of the other wolves had been arrested under false charges and the Blaze Ops helped them escape. "Sly and the others used to work out of the Magnus Academy, too. They did all sorts of undercover work against a terrorist organization—"

"Trevor," Clinton interrupted, sounding annoyed and exasperated at the same time. "That's not exactly something we're permitted to tell civilians."

Trevor flinched. He didn't like being chastised so he muttered, "We're technically civilians now, too."

"Now?" Jessica pressed, picking up on that one word. "You mean you weren't?"

Clinton let out a heavy sigh as he rolled to a sitting position. Trevor more sensed the movement than either heard or saw it. "Trev and I were in the military for a while, yes. Lucy signed up and so naturally, we followed her."

Jessica was silent for a moment, and then, "Do you love her?"

"Of course," Trevor said. "She practically raised us. She's like our big sister and mother all rolled into one."

"So you don't love her romantically?"

Trevor noted the hint of jealousy in Jessica's tone and a wicked grin spread over his face. He wanted to tease her about it but held himself back. She'd been stiff and cold to him and Clinton the past week. They had decided early on that there were too many risks to having sex again—they had to protect from being discovered out here—and once Jessica realized she couldn't change their minds no matter how hard she made it for them, she had withdrawn.

He didn't want to lead her on. It wasn't fair to her when he already knew she wanted a mate. So that meant that teasing was out of the question. It was too easy to fall into comfortable patterns and send the wrong signals.

"What's the plan, anyway?" Jessica murmured. "Are we going to go running all over the place constantly? Why can't we go back to the lake pocket? That was the perfect place to hide."

"It was a good temporary place but we're just lucky none of us had to use the bathroom while we were there," Trevor replied. "It was never meant to be long-term."

"Oh. I didn't think about that."

Trevor hummed, but it was Clinton who continued. "We have a good place that's well-hidden and secure that we're heading to. We just have to make sure that nobody's on our tail as we get there. Right now the plan is to shake that damn jaguar, and from there we'll get to our hideout. We ought to be able to stay there until the deadline is imminent. By then, the other shifters will have thinned each other out, and we'll have less competition to get to the drop zone and get our money."

Jessica rolled onto her stomach and cuddled deeper into her sleeping bag. "So… this hideout. It's not another underwater pocket, is it?"

"No," Clinton assured her, once more speaking before Trevor could. "It's a place that Sly showed us. Somewhere that he hid out when he'd been wrongfully accused of terrorism and was hiding out until he could clear his name. It's called the Rockery. Actually, that's apparently where he and Chloe met. In any case, we have stocked it with several months' worth of supplies and have already got a toilet area set up so we won't have to worry about being discovered."

"Well, not too much," Trevor chimed in.

Jessica let out an angry huff and her voice grew cold. "And what exactly do you intend to do with me during this time? Are you going to just lock me up? Keep me shackled to the wall? Or maybe you'll have me bound and gagged the entire time?"

Trevor sighed. He wanted to reassure her that everything was going to work out fine, but what they were after and what she was after were such different things! How could he reassure her without promising to find her a new mate or some such thing? It was impossible for all three of them to get what they wanted out of this competition.

Unless we take her as a mate, a small voice whispered in the back of his mind, and his wolf yipped slightly at the thought. Trevor paused, placing a hand over his chest. He hadn't heard his wolf get that excited about anything since… well, since they'd been in their underground pocket and Jessica started taking off her clothes.

"I thought you wanted to be bound and gagged," Clinton murmured. He'd stretched out on the floor again. No sleeping bag. If he got cold he'd just shift to his wolf form.

"Not like that," Jessica said and there was embarrassment in her tone. "I don't want… I shouldn't have told you about that. It was inappropriate and disgusting."

"Disgusting?" Trevor repeated. He searched the darkness outside as his brows pinched together. "Troubling, maybe. Unexpected. But you said that you want it only the way you want it, right? It's not like you want just any man to treat you like that. You want to be able to play and explore in a trusting situation."

Jessica was silent for a moment and then whispered, "Do I?"

"Don't you?"

Another moment of silence, followed by a heavy sigh. "Sorry. I shouldn't be putting all of this on you. You have no obligations to me, and I have no obligations to you.

We're not a couple or a threesome or… whatever. We're not committed, we're not in a relationship and I shouldn't put either of you on the spot like that."

Trevor struggled to know how to respond to that. Because on the one hand, yeah. It was a very uncomfortable conversation for him. He didn't know himself what sort of psychological and lifetime effects happened when a person was sexually assaulted, but he had empathy and could imagine it. He also knew that rape fantasies were pretty common. He'd found that out while doing research into BDSM and S&M and bondage play.

This, though. It was completely outside of his realm of knowledge. But he felt he had to say something. "If it's something that is really bothering you then maybe you should talk to someone about it. I know that Beth got William and Jacob to see a therapist. Maybe… maybe that's something you should think about."

"Tried that," Jessica's voice was like shattered glass, sharp and cutting. "It didn't help."

"Maybe you just didn't find the right one?" Trevor suggested.

"And maybe you need therapy," Jessica spat. "Maybe you—"

A loud thumping noise on the roof of the safehouse made them all fall silent. Trevor tensed, pushing himself away from the window. He kept an eye on the darkness as something huge and heavy scraped across the roof. It was too big to be a jaguar, even a bear or another wolf. He inhaled sharply, his heart pounding, and his wolf's hackles rising when he caught the thin smell of smoke.

He opened his mouth, but before he could warn them, red light flickered in the window. A roar echoed through the forest as flames scorched the cabin. A huge, clawed hand punched through the roof. Jessica screamed. Trevor lunged forward, shifting as he did so.

His teeth scraped against hard scales as Clinton seized Jessica. Smoke filled the cabin and the hand withdrew.

Clinton tossed Jessica onto Trevor's back and flung open the door, but the dragon was already waiting. Even as Trevor got Jessica clear of the burning building, a huge wing batted him. He shifted, wrapping his body around Jessica's and holding her head and neck steady as they were buffeted to the ground.

Clinton howled. The dragon roared back, then snatched Jessica up. Trevor snarled, clinging to her. A foot smacked into his chest and he went tumbling down.

"No," Jessica cried, but why, Trevor didn't know.

He shifted back to his wolf form. He and Clinton chased the dragon, following after its dark shadow until it was well gone. The scents faded to nothing and eventually, they pulled to a stop, well away from the burning cabin. Trevor's wolf howled in anger and desperation. It wanted to turn and attack Clinton. In the light of the moon, he saw his partner's eyes glittering.

They both shifted back to human form and Clinton swung at Trevor. "You were supposed to be watching!"

Trevor ducked under the blow. "It's not my fault that cabin only had one fucking window and the dragon came at us from the back."

A chuckle sounded overhead and both of them froze, then looked up. A black-haired man, his naked body covered in grease, dropped from the branches. Trevor instantly recognized his inky hair and green eyes. The jaguar. He snarled, about ready to attack, but the jaguar held up his hands in surrender.

"Well, this is an interesting turn of events," the jaguar said. "I'm Nikola, if you remember."

Trevor glared at him. He recognized the man now. He'd been at the last checkpoint. "What of it? Why have you been following us?"

"Because I'm a competitor in this competition, and I want to win the prize," Nikola replied sleekly. He smirked as he leaned against a tree. "So the dragon caught Jessica Byrd after all. This is an unfortunate turn of events, isn't it?

There's no way that any of us individually are going to be able to take on the king of the shifters."

Trevor flinched and Clinton growled at the reference to the dragon as a 'king'. The dragon that had taken them as slaves called himself a king. It left a bad taste in Trevor's mouth to have any other dragon called that. If this one likewise thought they were a king and acted the same way as the dragon who'd taken them slaves? His hands clenched. They had to get Jessica back and fast. Sure there were rules against mistreatment, but how was she supposed to prove mistreatment if the dragon didn't take her to the checkpoints?

"What do you want?" Clinton snapped.

Nikola smiled. "For us to help each other. I join your group. I help you keep Jessica and then when we're done, I get her, and you get the money. Simple."

Trevor tensed. He glowered at the jaguar. He wanted Jessica? Yes, she was sexy and smart and funny and amazing, but this jaguar couldn't possibly know that. He was looking at her as nothing but an object to be won. Trevor opened his mouth, his wolf's growls rising up his throat, but once more Clinton took control of the situation.

"Deal," he said.

Trevor could hardly believe what he was hearing. They couldn't just hand her over like that... but that was what Jessica wanted, wasn't it? She wanted a mate out of this contest. *And we can't give that to her.* So he was silent as Clinton and Nikola shook hands. This was what Jessica would want. And what she wanted... it was important, too.

CHAPTER NINE

Jessica wasn't sure whether it was because she hadn't had a chance to stop and breathe, whether it was from the fear of getting snatched by the dragon like this, or whether it was the swaying of the dragon back and forth on the winds, but by the time they landed, she promptly collapsed and vomited. It was only a little bit, but it burned on the way up. She hadn't managed to eat much, so tired from the long trip to that cabin, and now she felt a bit like death warmed over.

The dragon shifted back to human form as Jessica pushed herself to her knees. The first thing that she was surprised about was that this dragon was a woman, like the lionesses that had snatched her from the lakeside. The second was that the woman was still fully clothed. She frowned.

"Why do you still have clothes?" she blurted then flushed.

The dragon laughed a musical laugh as she helped Jessica to her feet. "Dragons have this special little ability," she said with a wry smile. "Out of all the shifters, we're the only ones who are able to shift our clothes with us. Call it magic. I do."

The woman winked at her, and then firmly pulled her toward a small greyish tent. It was pressed up against the sheer side of a cliff and had a border of boulders that were about three free high on every side of it.

That was when Jessica realized that the dragon had taken her to nearly the precipice of a mountain, and that mere feet from where she'd collapsed to vomit was an abrupt cutoff. In the darkness, there was no seeing anything beyond it and Jessica let out a short shriek, clutching at the dragon.

"Easy," the dragon said as she led Jessica into the tent and zipped it up behind them. "There. Can't see it now and it's not so scary."

Jessica was inclined to disagree, but her head was still spinning. She curled up against the far wall, feeling more secure with a hard rock on her back and beneath her. She swallowed hard as she looked up at the dragon, who slipped off her shoes and opened up a pack. Soon, a small LED lantern was turned on, filling the tent with cool light.

"Are you hungry?" the dragon asked gently. "Or maybe you'd just like to sleep? I know it's cold up here, but we can share."

The dragon looked up with a small, coy smile and Jessica had the sudden thought that she was not here for the same reason the lionesses had signed up. She swallowed hard as she shook her head slightly. "I don't think that will be a good idea."

The dragon considered her for a moment and then shrugged. "Alright. Well, I don't need a sleeping bag so you can have this one. You're shivering."

Jessica was cold, but she wasn't certain about the situation. This was the second time she had been snatched away from Trevor and Clinton, the second time she'd been terrified as she was taken away from them. Of course, they had terrified her when they first snatched her from that cabin, but she had somehow thought that all of this would happen differently.

At the same time, though, she was cold. What harm would it do to wrap up? She pulled the sleeping bag around her shoulders, watching the dragon.

"My name is Renee," the dragon pushed.

"Jessica."

Renee considered her for a moment and then sighed. "When you signed up for this you were told there was a possibility that a woman would claim you in the end, right?"

Jessica flushed. "Of course. I'm not... I'm bi," she said, then flushed. "Sorry. But you did sort of grab me in the middle of the night and burn down the house I was in and... this whole thing has been a little bit different than what I was expecting. I never expected Clinton and Trevor to be the first ones who..."

"The wolves?" Renee frowned. "You know them?"

Jessica hesitated. She would be just as happy with a female mate as she would a male mate, wouldn't she? She hadn't ever had a relationship with a woman before, never pursued one, either. It was a complicated part of her life that she honestly preferred not to think too much about. Her fantasies never included women, even though she would have the same physical reaction to a beautiful woman as she did a beautiful man.

Maybe that's my problem. Maybe I'm cutting myself off from too many potential partners and that's why I don't have anybody.

She shook her head sharply, trying to push out those thoughts. If Renee had her now, that meant that for the time being she belonged to the dragon. Who knew, maybe Renee was better prepared or had better defenses than Clinton and Trevor.

And if Renee won...

"I knew Clinton and Trevor from before the competition," Jessica finally said. She kept staring at the dragon. She was beautiful, with silver-blue eyes, long dark hair and a hint of an Irish accent. Beautiful. Sexy, with the type of body that Jessica wished she had and would turn her head on the street. "So it took me by surprise when they were... there."

Renee frowned heavily at that. "But you know that if I win this, you and I will be mated, right?"

"Well, yes…" Jessica frowned. "I don't really see why…?"

Renee huffed and looked away. "Sorry. I guess it's late, and I'm a little tired. I just didn't think that this would happen quite this way. Are the three of you…?"

Jessica unzipped her sleeping bag and got into a more comfortable position inside of it so she was a little warmer. Part of her wondered if she ought to go ahead and ask Renee to join her inside the bag, but for some reason, she was resistant to the idea. Maybe it was just because there was so much happening, and she still felt a little sick. Her brain felt like it was the last sock stuck on the inside of a washing machine.

"We're not in a relationship," Jessica finally said. "It's never going to be a relationship. They were very clear about that."

Renee's shoulders slumped. "But you wish there could be?"

"No," Jessica replied at once.

Renee rolled her eyes. "Please, Jessica. Maybe I've only known you for a few minutes, but I think I can recognize the signs. You said that way too quickly. You have the hots for them, don't you?"

Jessica let out an angry huff. "It's none of your business. Right now I'm not even registered to you. So you might have me, but there is no guarantee that you're going to win me. If you do, then we can talk about stuff like this."

Would Renee be willing to indulge in her secret, shameful fantasy? Jessica glanced away as she tried to picture herself with the beautiful dragon. But all it did was leave her with a bitter taste in her mouth—like she would be using Renee. Like Renee deserved better than this. She lay down in the sleeping bag, zipping it up now. Fuck. Why was it that as soon as she was away from Clinton and Trevor, and she had the chance to actually get a mate, she immediately started to wish that she was back with them?

Renee turned off the LED lantern. "Alright. After I've won you, then, you'll tell me?"

"Yeah. As long as you want to keep me." *But what if I don't want to keep her?*

Jessica hated the tangle of emotions in her chest as she shifted around, trying to get comfortable. The floor was covered in a thin mat that was better than the hardwood floor that Trevor and Clinton had her sleeping on, but not as comfortable as the bed in the cabin she'd first been in.

This wasn't what she wanted. This wasn't the breathless adventure of multiple people fighting for her that she had craved when she signed up for this competition. It was that stupid fucking prize money. It should never have been offered. Most of the people, if not all of them, were only after the million dollars and didn't want a mate.

Renee seems genuine, though. And if I am going to ask her to keep me, then I should start getting to know her, right? I should put in the effort. Maybe it is really soon… only a few minutes… but there is no point in delaying and hoping someone else will find me.

Anybody else would have the same problem. Renee, at least, didn't put off the creepy vibes that some of the people she'd seen at the last checkpoint had given off. She seemed to be genuine… Sure, seeing her attacking the lionesses had been a terrifying sight but…

Hmm. Maybe that is what I ought to bring up, then? Jessica took a deep breath. "When those lionesses had me and you attacked…"

Renee shifted to her side. "Did I frighten you?"

"Yes," Jessica said because there was no point in lying. "I was terrified to see you drop out of the sky like that and start to tear them up."

"I was just getting their implants."

"I know that now," Jessica replied. "I didn't know that at the time, and so it was scary."

Renee sighed. "I'm sorry that I frightened you. I'm not going to hurt you."

"Did you know that the lionesses only signed up in

protest? They thought this whole thing was sexist and objectifying and wanted to win me and the prize so they could use it to sue the sponsors."

Renee snorted.

"I'm sure they thought they were doing the right thing."

"I don't think they did their research. These competitions happen every year and they move through various genders for the prize. I appreciate their dedication, but their efforts were wasted." Renee moved a little closer again. "If this was sexist, then why are there so many women signed up as hunters?"

"I never said it was sexist."

A hand reached out, resting on her hand, then moved slowly up to her shoulder. "You're beautiful. You know that, right?"

Jessica was struck by the thought that she could have a happy life with Renee. Despite not really knowing her, and not knowing if she was after a mate or the prize money, Jessica could see a life with her. It would be stable and steady. Renee was dominant and determined, something Jessica liked in her partners. With a million-dollar prize, they could be quite comfortable. And if the way Renee was running her hand up and down Jessica's arm right now was any indication, she was interested in a physical, sexual relationship.

She'd probably be easier to keep up with than Clinton and Trevor.

But... it didn't feel like the happy ending it should have. If anything, it left Jessica cold on the inside. Maybe she wasn't as bi as she had thought?

"Well, we can talk more in the morning," Renee said as she withdrew her hand. "But you really shouldn't have signed up for this competition while you were pregnant."

Shock rushed over Jessica. "Pregnant? I'm not pregnant," she yelped.

Renee turned on the lantern again. "Aren't you?"

"N—" Jessica started, then stopped. When had her last period been? So much had happened over the last few months that she hadn't really paid attention… The blood drained from her face. The last time she remembered Aunt Flo visiting was almost three months ago. Her mouth opened and closed.

With a sigh, Renee pushed herself up. "Stay here and rest," she ordered. "I'm going to go get you a pregnancy test."

Jessica couldn't even protest. The words stopped in her throat as her mind turned over the possibility that she was pregnant… and she had no idea what she would do if it turned out that she was.

CHAPTER TEN

Clinton's wolf snarled deep in his chest, the sound vibrating through him. It took all of his efforts not to just snarl along with it. This whole situation was so utterly fucked up! He should not be teamed up with some random jaguar and hunting a dragon to get Jessica back from said dragon. This hit too close to home. He didn't care that Sly had all those dragon friends, and he didn't care what this dragon wanted or the fact that it was doing the same thing that Trevor and Clinton were doing.

All he saw was yet another dragon thinking that they ruled the world. Thinking that they deserved everything they wanted for no more reason besides the fact that they wanted it. An entitled, greedy bastard that needed to be taken down a peg or two.

Beside him, Trevor kept shooting him concerned looks that Clinton ignored. He didn't need Trevor to be all overly concerned about him. The situation was what it was. There was no point in freaking out about it.

Of course, that was easier said than done. Right, so Trevor had a good reason to be concerned.

Clinton shook his head. They had a fairly good idea of where the dragon had taken Jessica, at least, if they could believe Nikola. He wouldn't say how he got his information, just in case they double-crossed him, but he assured them that it was all on the level and that he knew. It wasn't exactly someone that inspired trust, but at the moment it was the best they had.

For now, though, they were stuck in camp, cooking some of the freeze-dried food they'd brought along with them. Luckily, they were near a creek which meant that they had enough water for the night and to refill their canteens for tomorrow but all the same. Clinton would rather have been out there still going through the night rather than waiting here.

Nikola could see how restless they were. "I'm surprised the two of you got so attached to our little Byrd so quickly," he mentioned, lounging lazily on the other side of the fire.

Clinton glanced up, annoyed. "What do you mean by that?"

"I mean," Nikola said slowly with an obvious smirk. "You two don't strike me as the type to accept help very easily and yet here we are. You must be desperate to get her back."

Clinton snorted and pulled the food off the fire. He had no business learning anything about them. He could go ahead and wonder all he wanted.

"We know her," Trevor said, looking utterly relaxed for Jessica being out there in the hands of a dragon. Not to mention letting his lips flap and revealing things he shouldn't be talking about. "We've known her for a few years and—"

"Shut up," Clinton snapped at him.

Nikola laughed softly.

Shooting him a glare, Clinton started eating. He had only gotten a few mouthfuls in, though, before a shiver passed down his spine. He leapt to his feet, a snarl in his throat. Even as he did so, a tiger leapt from the trees. It bellowed a challenge, landing lightly next to the fire and leaping at

Nikola. The jaguar shifted and slipped away.

A bear and lion both burst from the trees, coming at Clinton and Trevor. The wolves shifted and leapt out of the way of the initial charge. Their food scattered, plates flung this way and that. The bear took a moment, huffing, to knock the pot back into the fire—petty fucker! Clinton howled with fury as he leapt onto the bear's back, only to be knocked off by the lion. Trevor grabbed the lion's leg, yanking back hard.

The lion whirled, a huge paw patting Trevor and sending him over his head. Clinton growled as he focused on the bear, snapping at its face to try to drive it away. But these shifters had no intention of being driven away like Nikola had been. They fought hard, and soon fur scattered the ground and blood leaked from various injuries.

Clinton locked his teeth around the bear's arm, feeling the click of the implant beneath his jaws. He tore, trying to rip the implant out. Only something huge and heavy jumped on his back, pinning him down. The tiger was back, its huge jaws clenched on the scruff of Clinton's neck. He tried to shake it off, but the tiger was twice his size, and after the fight, he couldn't throw it.

The tiger bore down on him, forcing him to collapse in the dirt. Nearby, the lion had Trevor likewise pinned. The bear shifted back to his human form and pulled a small pack from the belt around his waist. A triumphant smirk crossed his face as he drew out a scalpel.

"Two more down," the bear crowed. "Shift back to human form and make this easy on yourselves."

He intended to cut out their implants. Clinton growled low in his throat, trying to dislodge the tiger again but to no avail.

The bear waited a moment and then shrugged. He headed for Trevor first. Trevor bucked, but the lion held him that much tighter. Anger and fear swept through Clinton. If their implants were removed, they were out of this competition. How were they supposed to save Jessica then? How were they going to get the money for the pack? A growl surged through him and he threw his head backward, forcing the tiger back, and then lunged forward. Pain burned through his neck as he choked himself on his own skin, his scruff stretching out behind it. The tiger's teeth tore through his hide, its grip loosened.

Clinton wiggled his way free and lunged at the bear, his teeth snapping. The bear let out a surprised yell and jumped out of the way. Clinton ignored him, jumping onto the lion's back. The tiger rammed them both, and they fell off of Trevor. Trevor jumped to his feet, whipping around to bite the tiger's face. The bear howled as it shifted—

And then a high-pitched, stinging noise swarmed Clinton's ears. He yelled out in pain as the noise like a thousand bees rang in his head. They stabbed into his brain, the agony making his vision whiteout. His wolf yelped, howled in pain, and then retreated. In human form, the sound was not quite so bad, but it still burned. Clinton slapped his hands over his ears, yelling for it to stop.

When it finally did stop, Clinton, Trevor, and their three attackers lay in their human forms on the ground, all panting and shivering from the sudden assault. Nikola strode back in, draped in a black cloth to hide his nakedness. A smile was on his lips as he came to stand over them. In his hand was a small black box, safety earmuffs on his head. He dropped a pair to Clinton and one to Trevor, which they both hurriedly put on.

"Now, how about we all stop fighting?" Nikola called. "Or I can turn this on and leave it here while I and my new friends here leave."

Clinton scrambled to his feet, putting distance between him and the other shifters so they couldn't steal his earmuffs. His head throbbed dully, and he had no intention of being subjected to that noise again. He glared at the black box and Nikola suspiciously.

The bear held up his hands. "What the hell is that thing?"

"Sonic emitter," Nikola replied with an impish grin. "If

you're looking for the girl with us, she's not here."

The lion got to his feet, followed closely by the tiger. The tiger rubbed his jaw and glared at the three of them. "What are you working with these two wolves for? Us cats have to stick together."

Nikola rolled his eyes. "Right, because I really want to put my chances in the hands of a tiger. You guys are solitary to the last. At least wolves have a pack mentality. And for your information, I'm with them because we have an agreement. The girl was taken by a dragon."

"A dragon?" the lion blurted. He threw his hands in the air, looking disgusted. "Well there's no point in this anymore is there? We can't take on a fucking dragon."

"Then leave and good riddance," Clinton snapped. His hands clenched. If they all left he'd be just fine with that. He didn't want them here. He needed to go after Jessica, to get her away from that fire-breathing lizard and to get her back to Deville safely. He was certain there were internet dating sites where she could find a decent guy to be with.

Not to mention a million dollars. That might not go as far as it once did, but it would go pretty far in preparing for the children's futures. If he was going to be part of the pack at Devil Mountain, then he was going to do his part to help them. There were so many kids already, and more on the way. He wanted them all to have the chances in life that he'd never gotten.

But for right now, he couldn't let himself get distracted. The shifters could attack at any moment and that tiger was eyeing Nikola right now.

"Right." Nikola nodded, still holding the box aloft. "This is going to be quite beneficial, isn't it? I take it the three of you have joined forced to collect Jessica and win the prize money? What's most important to you, the girl or the million dollars?"

The bear and lion glanced at each other, but the tiger snorted. "The money, of course! What good is a woman who signs up for something like this? She's probably a thrill-seeker and will move onto the next thrill as soon as she's bored. Not to say it wouldn't be fun to pass her around a bit—"

Clinton snarled. He would have launched himself forward except Trevor grabbed him and held him back. From Trevor's face, it was a difficult thing for him to do. Clinton's hands clenched into fists. He trembled with the effort to keep himself in human form. His wolf growled and snapped, wanting to taste the tiger's blood and teach it a lesson about respecting Jessica.

"There will be no passing her around," Nikola said pleasantly. "Even if the three of you were to get her. You see, she's mated to these two."

Clinton's snarls faded. He worked to keep the surprise off his face as he glanced at Nikola from the corner of his eye. What was he playing at?

"If you join us, then together the six of us can take down the dragon. Then we get Jessica and we hold her until it's time to collect our reward. Clint and Trev here get the girl as they want—"

"She's not mated," the tiger blurted. His hair stood on end. "Why would she sign up if she was already mated?"

Clinton opened his mouth but even as he started to snap that it was none of the tiger's business, Nikola sighed.

"Her parents. You see, Clinton and Trevor here," Nikola walked behind them, tucking away the black box. "They're from poor stock. Orphans who grew up on the streets. Never even finished high school. Not good enough in their eyes for their only daughter. But when they heard about this competition, they said if Clint and Trev could win, they'd give their blessing. So you see, they have no interest in a million-dollar prize."

Clinton closed his mouth and glared at Nikola. *Stay calm.*

"Splitting it four ways is better than getting burnt to a crisp by a dragon," Nikola said with a nonchalant shrug. "And I know where she took our Jessica."

She? Clinton frowned at him. The dragon was a woman? How did Nikola know that?

But it didn't really matter. The other shifters agreed to these terms and before he knew it, Clinton was part of a coalition. Their new teammates laughed about the havoc they'd wrecked, the bear apologizing for ruining their pot. Trevor took it all in stride, laughing with them, getting into cleaning up the mess as though there were no problems here.

Clinton did not have the same tender feelings toward their newfound allies. He glared at them all, hating each and every one of them. They were just three more people who could stab them in the back. But he hardly had a choice now, did he? So he shut his mouth, cleaned up camp, and started a new meal while calculating just how far their supplies would last with an extra three mouths to feed.

CHAPTER ELEVEN

The last place Trevor expected to find a dragon was in an old, run-down house. Somehow, he'd never envisioned dragons surrounding themselves by anything other than gold and finery. This house, though, had seen better days. He was also surprised that the dragon had brought Jessica somewhere so easily accessible and so close to human settlements. With her wings, the dragon ought to have been perched up at the top of a treacherous mountain.

"Are you sure this is where she is?" Clinton asked Nikola under his breath. The jaguar and Trevor had scouted on ahead earlier, during the daylight. There was no sign of any sort of cameras or security. It was just the house, and Jessica inside of it.

Trevor had seen the dragon—smaller than he had thought she'd be, bringing Jessica a glass of lemonade as they sat on a set of plastic yard chairs just outside the house. Almost like she was flaunting Jessica. It was just like a dragon to be so arrogant as to think that she was untouchable. Baiting them to come in.

Trevor licked his lips, nodding slightly to Clinton in answer to his question. This wasn't so simple as it appeared to be, he knew that. But his wolf was impatient and eager to get to Jessica. With the other shifters pressing around it was setting him on edge, which was not something that he was used to feeling. Normally, Trevor was pretty confident in whatever it was he chose to do. Normally, he didn't feel conflicted about any course of action when he set his mind to it.

This though... On the one hand, he was very eager to get Jessica back. But on the other, he couldn't help but think that any of these shifters would gladly put a knife in his back.

There was little time for doubts, though. The group spread out, surrounding the house. Lights were still on inside and Jessica and the dragon were in the main room, eating something and laughing together. A twinge of doubt made Trevor pause. What if this was what Jessica wanted? What if she had found the mate she wanted so badly?

Then they can be together once this competition is over, he told himself firmly. *After Clinton and I have the money.*

Nikola whistled, the signal to attack. Trevor pushed aside his doubts and charged up the steps. He threw open the door for Clinton and the lion to slip into the house. The bear roared from against one of the windows, drawing the dragon's attention. The dragon hardly looked up from her meal as she stood. Her movements were lazy, and Jessica sighed as she stood.

"I told you, eight o'clock on the dot," the dragon purred. "Run upstairs, Jessie, while I take care of these brutes."

The lion and tiger both rushed the dragon while the bear disappeared, rounding the house to get to the door. But as Trevor was about to launch himself in there and help, Nikola slinking up the stairs after Jessica caught his eye. He yipped to Clinton, and the two of them took off after the jaguar. The stairs were too narrow for wolf form, so they shifted to human form. They arrived just in time to see Nikola slinging Jessica over his shoulders and launching himself out the window.

The sounds of fighting echoed up the stairs, but Trevor didn't care. With his wolf howling, he threw himself out the window after them. He shifted mid-air, landing on all four paws. The jaguar took off into the woods, Trevor close on his tail. He snapped out a warning, telling Nikola to stop. Clinton leapt in the shadows to one side, following after.

Trevor put on a burst of speed, slapping Nikola's legs out from him. He dove for Jessica as she tumbled off the jaguar's back. Shifting back to human form, he grabbed Jessica, rolling with her to prevent her from getting beat up. They stopped with his back smacking hard into a tree, and there he lay, gasping for breath with Jessica in his arms.

And his wolf had never been happier.

"Ouch," Jessica muttered. Her hands tightened on Trevor's shoulders and she looked up into his eyes for a brief moment before she turned her face away.

He released her and scrambled to his feet as Clinton loomed over Nikola, snarling blackly. Nikola rolled to his belly until Clinton backed off, and then he jumped to his feet, shifting fluidly to human form as he did so. Seconds later the lion, tiger, and bear were with them, dragging the dragon along. She had a bloody forearm. The implant was removed.

"You weren't going to double-cross us, were you?" the tiger snarled, glaring at Clinton rather than any of the others. "The plan was—"

"Of course, we weren't double-crossing anybody," Nikola interrupted smoothly. He smiled as he stepped over to Jessica. "But she was getting away. We can't get our prize if we don't have our prize now, can we?"

Trevor let out a snort. The jaguar had been planning on double-crossing them. It was plainly obvious. But he wasn't going to fight about it right now. The dragon was taken care of, which meant that he had to worry about the others now. And Nikola always seemed to know exactly what was happening.

"Well," the tiger said, satisfied by Nikola's words. He glanced over Jessica. "You are juicier than I thought you'd be. Can I have her first or are we drawing straws."

A snarl ricocheted from Trevor's throat at the same time Clinton growled. They both closed in around Jessica, blocking her from the tiger's view. Here, the dragon chuckled. "What makes you think she wants that, Tiger?"

The tiger turned a glare on the dragon. "That's what this competition is about. She knew what she was getting into when she signed up. When we have her, she belongs to us. Those are the rules. She wouldn't have signed up if she didn't want to be fucked by every contestant."

Jessica made a protesting noise in her throat, and Trevor very nearly launched himself at the tiger. It was only the smirk on Nikola's face that stopped him. It would play right into the jaguar's hands to start fighting, lose sight of Jessica, and let Nikola spirit her away.

Beside him, Clinton growled out, "A woman, or any person for that matter, is allowed to change their minds. Besides, what about the competition said that she had to be willing to let any person who touched her fuck her? Keep your suggestions to yourself, Tiger. If you want to have sex with Jessica, then you can fucking *ask* her."

Trevor nodded, flexing his muscles as he looked at the three of them. Nikola had wandered over to the dragon and was now looking a little bored.

The dragon cleared her throat. "Besides that, Jessica has something she needs to tell you. Don't you, Jessie?"

"Oh, shut up!" Jessica snapped. Her arms were wrapped tightly around herself and she glared at all of them. Her gaze focused on the tiger and her lips pulled back in a damn convincing snarl. "All of you just shut up as though I'm not here. For your information, no, I did not sign up for this competition to be fucked by every person who happened to have me for a few hours. This was meant to be a competition for contestants to find a mate. Not just have sex and throw me away!"

Trevor flinched. Was that what she thought he and Clinton were doing? Having sex and then throwing her away? Yeah, they didn't plan to make anything permanent out of this, but they weren't just tossing her aside like garbage... were they?

"You forget something," Nikola put in here. "Clinton and Trevor are already her mates. You get the money; they get the girl."

Jessica jerked, her eyes widening. Trevor flinched again. She was going to blow this, wasn't she?

"I don't believe it," the tiger shot back. "I think the three of you are looking to con the rest of us. If she really was their mate, they wouldn't have told me to ask her before fucking."

"Or maybe we just trust her," Clinton spat back. His muscles were tense as he shifted from foot to foot, looking like he wanted to attack. "The sexual agreements the three of us have is none of your fucking business."

"She is not your mate," the tiger said, inching forward. His eyes remained on Jessica, and Trevor had to remind himself that attacking with the intent to kill was not going to help anybody here. "I don't care what you're playing at, either. She's juicy and I want her. Oh, pardon me." He bowed sarcastically. "Will you do me the honor of spreading your legs for me, my lady?"

Trevor had to grab Clinton's arm as he made to leapt forward. The lion and bear both tensed, their lips pulling back in snarls. The air was thick with tension, Jessica shivering behind the wolves while Nikola inexplicably smirked. Beside him, the dragon started to laugh.

"You seem to be very determined," she drawled, and Trevor hated the sound of her voice. Why was she still here? She should be gone already. But she was smiling and that set his fur on edge. "I can assure you, Mr. Tiger, that Jessie is mated to these two. If you need proof, just get her a pregnancy test. She's carrying their child."

Shock swept through Trevor. He was halfway to protesting before it even fully sank in. His mind reeled as he turned to stare at Jessica. Her hands were clutched tightly before her, her eyes wide and her skin pale. Bracing herself for his reaction. Beside him, Clinton was stiff as a board. Trevor didn't spare him a glance, but the confusion rolling off him was blinding.

His wolf was going crazy. Running in circles, gnawing at his ribs, play bowing with its tail wagging like crazy. Even if Trevor didn't know how he was supposed to feel about this news—it couldn't be real, could it—at the same time, there was some strange elation rushing through him.

He never had thought of himself as a fatherly type. He was perfectly happy being an uncle to Tanya. Sure there were times when he thought it would be nice to have kids of his own, but the sort of people that he and Clinton were… they didn't know how to look after kids. Didn't know how to be fathers. Besides that, you needed a mate to have kids. But it didn't work that way in real life. Having sex with most women could end up with them being pregnant. They hadn't been as careful with Jessica as they should have been. He swallowed hard as he struggled to focus on the situation.

The tiger was having a fit, with the bear and lion both talking him down, reminding him of the money. Trevor briefly wondered what the nature of their relationship was, but he really didn't care. The dragon, looking rather pleased with herself, told Jessica to call her if things didn't happen the way she wanted and sauntered away, having sowed enough seeds of dissent for her liking.

Nikola looked somewhat disappointed but only asked once whether it was true. Trevor still didn't know what to think. It'd been three months since he, Clinton and Jessica had had sex in Deville. Three months… that was a long time for her to keep it secret.

Was she really concerned about us not being serious with her, or is it that she doesn't want us? Trevor swallowed hard. He would understand if she didn't... it wasn't as though either he or Clinton had any real prospects right now. Nor did they have much ambition in life...

Clinton turned abruptly toward Jessica. He grabbed her wrist. "We need to talk," he snapped, and then pulled her into the trees.

CHAPTER TWELVE

Jessica chewed her lip and Clinton pulled her away from the others. Trevor followed after, a dazed look on his face that she didn't like. Why had Renee blurted it out like that? She knew that Jessica was surprised by the pregnancy, too, so why did she think it was a good idea to tell all these men?

I should have had the opportunity to tell Trevor and Clinton first. Jessica shivered, her stomach acidic. But then again, that tiger... the way he'd looked at her, his tone, his words. He didn't seem like the kind who would respect her saying no unless she had a man there backing her up. Her heart twisted as she thought about it. *Isn't that what I want, though?* She closed her eyes as Clinton came to a stop, finally releasing her wrist. *No. That isn't what I want. I want to play a game with someone I trust. I don't want some random man deciding when my no isn't good enough. I want to be with a man who will make sure that we are in the correct time and place to play those games.*

She opened her eyes to find Clinton and Trevor both glaring at her. Her heart skipped a beat and then started to ache. She still couldn't believe it—pregnant. With their child. Now what were they going to do? What were they going to think? This whole situation was so complicated, she didn't know what she was supposed to be feeling or thinking. Her hands clutched at each other as she stared back at the two of them.

"I didn't know," she started, but then Clinton embraced her. Jessica tensed, but when Trevor wrapped his arms around her as well, the tension just melted from her body.

For the first time in a long, long time, she allowed herself to feel safe and warm in their embrace. Maybe they did want her. Maybe this wasn't as bad as she thought. Maybe they would be able to—

"The others are watching," Clinton murmured into her ear. "So we have to pretend like we really are mates, understood."

Jessica closed her eyes as the warmth faded, replaced by a cold ache in her heart. So that was it. This wasn't a comforting embrace. It was a lie to continue the lies they'd told those other shifters. Jessica wanted to pull away but didn't. What would be the point of doing that?

Trevor's lips were against her ear, hiding them from the others so they couldn't read his lips. "Are you really pregnant, Jessica?"

Jessica nodded, letting them hold her because she wanted to hold onto some semblance of feeling safe even though she knew that it was impossible now. "I am."

Clinton let out a soft noise, and she didn't know what to make of it. They'd be running the math in their heads right now. It was too early to tell from their playtime down in the lake-pocket, so it had to be in Deville. And that was three months ago. Were they assuming that she knew all this time? That she'd been keeping it a secret from them? She swallowed heavily. Would they believe her if she told them that she hadn't realized she was pregnant? They didn't know what her body was like, they didn't know that she never kept track of her period anyway.

"Is it ours?" Clinton growled.

Actually growled. As though daring her to say it was. Her

shoulders stiffened, her spine going straight. There was no need to use that tone! Regardless of the situation, there wasn't any reason for him to be angry with her, certainly not before she had a chance to explain it all.

"Well?" he hissed, sounding even angrier.

It was that tone that made Jessica lie. "No," she breathed. Her tone was icy in comparison, and she pulled away from them both. So what if they had lies that they wanted the other shifters to believe? They had no right to treat her like this.

She caught a disappointed look on Trevor's face, but she ignored it. If he was so disappointed then he could have been the one to talk first so that his partner didn't treat her like a piece of shit. Her hands clenched at her sides as she glared at first one and then the other. She thought about raising her voice to let the other shifters know that they were being lied to, but the thought of that tiger made her stop short.

"It's not yours," she breathed instead. "And it's none of your business who the father is, either. You're not in this competition for me so it doesn't matter. If you want to pretend like we're mates, I'll pretend with you, but I expect a cut of the money at the end. Understood?"

Both of them looked a little startled, but Jessica raised her chin. She wasn't going to go through all of this with nothing to show for it. And she was pregnant... she needed to be able to pay for everything that went with that!

Both of the wolves gave her looks that she knew all too well. The crafty, cunning sort of looks that men always gave her. Whatever self-esteem she had curled up and died right there, followed quickly by a sense of utter self-loathing. What had she been thinking? Why had she gone and said something like that? Why had she been so confrontational about it?

What difference did it make if they knew that her baby was fathered by one of them? The only thing she could think of was that maybe they would be even more determined to keep her from the other shifters. Maybe they would want to keep her after the competition was over.

She did this all the time. She was always sabotaging herself. It wasn't just with romantic relationships, either. Instead of thanking Beth and the other women in Deville for their concern and letting them see what protections had been put in place for this competition, she had simply lied to them. Sure she had every intention of keeping in contact with them after she got her mate but... but a lie like that would weigh on any relationship.

Lifting a hand, she covered her eyes as she tried to figure out what she was supposed to be doing here. Maybe she deserved to be thrown away since she seemed to be determined to always throw herself away. Her shoulders started to shake, and she almost hoped that the two wolves would put their arms around her again.

It would make them walking away hurt all the worse, she knew that, but having their arms around her felt so good. It felt safe, something she hadn't felt in what seemed like forever.

"Jessica," Clinton murmured, his voice so low she could hardly hear him. "Don't lie to us. Is this our baby?"

Yes, her heart cried, but her mouth said, "I already told you, no. Why would I lie about this? Let's just get through this competition. It was a stupid idea to sign up in the first place."

Trevor looked... disappointed. Jessica tried not to look at him. She didn't want to know why he would be disappointed. There were too many other things going on and besides that, it wasn't like they were going to be honest with her anyway. Not when people were watching them. They couldn't have a true, honest discussion when they were being spied on.

Apparently, we can't have an honest discussion when I'm involved, either.

"What did you tell them?" she asked then because they

needed to have their stories straight.

"Just how your parents don't approve of us since we're poor," Trevor said. The disappointment washed from his face, settling on a careful mask as he took her hand in his. "And they told us that they'd give us their blessing if we proved our devotion to you."

So they were pretending that they were already in a relationship. That it wasn't just a thing that started with the competition. She nodded slowly, showing that she understood. Although how they were going to continue this, she didn't know. Or, judging by the look on Clinton's face, if they were even going to want to continue the lie.

But then the anger disappeared, and he sighed heavily, embracing her. "Just as long as that dragon didn't hurt you."

Jessica leaned into the embrace, partly for the show of it, partly because she really did crave that contact. Maybe when this was all over and they had the money, she would be able to tell them, and she'd know better where they stood with each other. They couldn't have a deep talk while they were being watched, she couldn't ask them if they wanted to keep her now or not.

But I'm not going to get any money, am I? she thought with a sinking heart. *The other shifters are getting the money now.*

No, that wasn't right... Clinton and Trevor wanted that money. They were determined to get it. So this whole thing had to be a ruse of some sort. Keeping the other shifters on their side, helping them until they could get away. Yes, that had to be it. Which meant, sooner or later, they were going to make a break for it.

She just hoped that they would let her in on the plan first, so she wasn't caught by surprise. And who knew? Maybe one of those shifters would turn out to be the mate she wanted. If not, then she always had Renee that she could call up once this was all over. Right? Maybe she needed to try a relationship with a woman. She'd never given it a try, but she was certain it would be pretty straightforward...

right?

Jessica shook her head as she rubbed her temples. "There is too much happening right now. I can't keep my head on straight."

"We'll get going, then. We can't camp here; there will be too many other hunters after us." Trevor took her hand and lead her back through the trees to where the others waited.

All of these men were naked, she realized. Somehow it hadn't registered. Not even when the wolves were hugging her. Weird. Was she that out of it or was she adjusting to all the nudity? The tiger looked put-out and she avoided looking at him altogether. If he had grabbed her alone, would he have pressed the situation?

And if I hadn't slept with Trevor and Clinton and then found out I was pregnant, would I want to sleep with him? He was just as attractive as the other shifters. Muscular, tattooed, exuding power. Was it just how he had approached the situation regarding sex that put her off or was it because she didn't want anybody to touch her who wasn't Trevor and Clinton?

If that was the case, if she couldn't stand the thought of anybody else touching her, she was well and truly fucked. The wolves had made it clear that they didn't want her. If her body craved them and nobody else, then how was she ever supposed to be satisfied in life again?

The men all shifted back to their animal forms and Jessica climbed onto Trevor's back. With the way Clinton had been looking at her, she didn't want to rely on him right now. She had a feeling that he needed space.

Maybe when this was over, she would return to Deville. She had a job there. She had friends. It was bland and lifeless, but she could find a way to make it work for her. It would be a nice place to raise a child, and by then Clinton and Trevor would know the truth. And maybe they'd have sleepovers. They could be friends with benefits. And if the baby was a shifter, it would be good to be near the pack…

But in her heart, Jessica knew that it wouldn't work like that. That this pregnancy only meant one thing—but she was not ready to think about giving her child up. Not yet.

CHAPTER THIRTEEN

The Rockery, as Sly called it, was deep within the woods. Nobody would be able to just happen to find it. From the outside, it looked like a solid rock rising from a heavily wooded forest straight into the sky. From above, it looked like a sheer drop. From either side, rock, rock, rock. It was only after you passed through the narrow fissure—something you couldn't see until you were inside of it—that you saw that there was more to this cliff than what you could see.

A small space was open from the cliff face to the wall, big enough for stretching out and doing some light exercises. From there, several rooms had been carved into the cliff. They went deep enough to give each of the contestants their own space, which had the added benefit of them not killing each other.

Clinton was not so certain that their 'teammates' didn't plan to try to snatch Jessica and cut out their implants, but so far everything seemed to be in order. They were satisfied that Jessica, Clinton and Trevor were mates. Her pregnancy—which they had checked and double-checked—was the final clincher in that. Even Nikola seemed convinced even though he was the one who made it up in the first place.

Still.

He sighed as he checked over their supplies. He and Trevor had planned for three people staying here for four months. Yes, things had delayed a little, but they now had seven people living here and their supplies were going faster than intended. They were going to have to hunt, which was why he was leaving with the bear, Matthew, and Nikola to do some hunting.

Jessica was pregnant and they could not have her going hungry... it was bad enough that they weren't taking her to see a doctor regularly.

His wolf yipped, that familiar sense of anger and excitement rising in him. His wolf couldn't seem to understand that she wasn't pregnant with his child. It was happy and excited every time he saw her. It wanted to stay with her, sniffing at her neck and skin to detect the subtle signs of pregnancy. It wanted him to run his hands over her belly, which was starting to get rounder, and to kiss her again and again until there was no space between them.

It kept waking him up in the middle of the night, thinking about what additions they'd need to add to the cabin for a baby. To think about how to research schools. To talk with the other fathers in the pack about what it meant to be a dad

But he wasn't the father. His wolf needed to accept that.

Even now, it urged him to go to her. For the two weeks that they had been here at the Rockery, he had managed to get it to cool its jets a bit, to pull back and not feel the need to be constantly at Jessica's side. His mind would turn to her constantly, even when he was trying to figure out a way to get away from these guys and get back to a situation where he was in control. In truth, he knew that everything was so far out of his control that no amount of planning could change that.

Jessica was pregnant. And for a few glorious minutes, he had thought that he was going to be a father. Even though the panic had threatened to strangle him, since he had no idea where to even start being a dad, it had been such elation. Then she had told them the father of her child wasn't either one of them. And that should have been the end of it. He had no claim over her, and he appreciated that she was being honest with them, rather than lying and trying to use that to her advantage in all of this.

Maybe it would have been better if they had actually been able to have a real talk. But they couldn't. Not with these other shifters hanging around.

And that made him so angry. Not that they were there—although that didn't help—but that Jessica would sign up for something like this knowing she was pregnant. It was stupid and reckless. She knew that she was being hunted, she knew that this competition would involve people fighting over her. It was all too easy for shifters to lose control for one moment, and they could hurt her. To be pregnant and put herself in that situation made it all the worse.

A shuffling behind him made him turn. He knew it was her even before he saw her beautiful face. His muscles stiffened as his wolf danced with delight. "Jessica. I thought you were resting."

"Trevor told me that you think I knew I was pregnant before coming out here," she said in that blunt way of hers. "Is that why you've been growling and snapping at everybody these past two weeks?"

Clinton's lips pressed together.

Jessica let out a heavy sigh as she rolled her eyes. "Of course it is. Because why talk to me and ask when you can mope around about it."

Clinton's frown increased. That wasn't the behavior that mates were supposed to have with each other. Or was it? He didn't know what to do with this whole complicated scheme. It would be better if they could just get rid of the other shifters and take Jessica somewhere else that was just as fortified as this place. That wasn't going to happen, though. There was no way he and Trevor could manipulate the others into turning against each other, and they couldn't take on four other shifters, not when they were all watching each other so carefully.

But whatever. Right now he could at least discuss this situation. Because even mates could lie to each other, right. "Alright. Yes. I am angry with you. What were you thinking, agreeing to this shitstorm when you're pregnant?"

"I didn't know, Clinton," she said softly. "I don't keep track of when I have my periods. I never have. I didn't even think about it until Renee said that I was pregnant. I don't even know how she figured it out. Because I sure didn't know."

Clinton considered her for a moment. His wolf growled at him and he decided that, just this once, he was going to believe her. It was a crazy, messed-up situation they were in, and he was tired of constantly being on guard. So he let his shoulders drop, nodded, and managed a smile for her. She blinked several times as she stared at him like it was that unusual to see him smile.

Was it?

"Thanks for telling me," he said. "And I'm sorry for moping instead of asking you."

Here, she returned his smile tentatively. "Good. I'm glad."

"I'm about to head out hunting," he said, moving to take her hand, in part because his wolf wanted him to, in part to play the game. "Are you going to be okay here with Trevor? We're leaving Carlos and Oliver here."

A scowl crossed her face at the mention of Oliver, the tiger. He had been relentless about moaning that she shouldn't have signed up if she didn't want to have sex with every man in existence. Clinton had eventually shut him up by punching him in the face, but that didn't stop his sulking.

"I'll be fine with Trevor," she said slowly. "Just take care of yourself, okay?"

"I will." He smiled again and for a brief moment, the knots of tension drained away.

But then he remembered that she wasn't his mate, it was just an act, and he wasn't her baby's father. Neither was Trevor. They weren't going to have anything to do with her or the baby after this competition was over and so there was no use in getting attached. So he stepped away, nodded once at her, and went to join Matthew and Nikola on their hunting trip.

He was distracted and irritable, but between the three of them, they were able to bring down a moose. It would be enough to feed them for a while, at least, although they needed to prepare the meat before taking it back to camp. A fire would give away their location, after all. So, they cooked up the meat where they'd felled the moose, packing the cooked meat into containers that they shoved into a stream to cool down.

Nikola headed back to the Rockery to grab a cooler, in which they'd be able to store the meat. It would keep it good for a while at least. Long enough for them to eat it.

It did mean that Clinton and Matthew were left alone. Clinton would have been fine with that—except Matthew decided that he had to make *small talk*. Clinton's hackles rose. He hated small talk. If people didn't have anything important to say, they should just keep their mouths shut and not bother everyone else with their chatting.

"You're a lucky man," the bear said as he turned a chunk of meat over the fire. "That Jessica. She is one helluva woman."

Clinton grunted at him.

"I didn't sign up for a mate, I was more interested in the money," Matthew continued, "but it's been… interesting. Being around her. If she wasn't already taken, I certainly would want to have a chance with her."

Clinton continued to ignore him as he cut up the last chunks of meat into more manageable sizes. He didn't want to talk about Jessica with Matthew. Or anybody else, for that matter. It was none of their business. They needed to just shut up and leave him, Trevor, and Jessica alone.

But would Jessica want Matthew? She didn't sign up for the money in this competition. She wanted a mate. She wanted to have someone who she could come home to, someone she could share her life with. Had those plans changed since she learned she was pregnant? She and that dragon seemed to be quite friendly for how little time they had spent together...

Clinton hadn't asked her about that. He'd just assumed that it was some sort of thing like the lionesses had been. But then, Renee had told her to call her... was there something more there? Jessica hadn't told him if she was bi or pan—he didn't think she would be a lesbian, although he supposed there were plenty of lesbians who slept with men before they realized their own sexuality—but it wasn't like Jessica had any reason to tell him either. Her sexuality was her own business. He had no right to start asking those questions. They didn't have a relationship, so she had no obligations to tell him.

But if she did want to be Renee's mate, she should have said something by now.

Clinton shook his head. Why would she? He cleared his throat, wanting to silence the runaround thoughts in his brain as well as calm his wolf as it paced and growled. It wanted to get back to the Rockery, to get back to Trevor and Jessica and to curl up with the two of them. He was struck suddenly by how tired he was. His muscles were sore, his entire body just lacking any energy.

"Just saying you're a lucky guy," Matthew said, and Clinton realized he'd been growling. "I'm not looking to step on your toes or nothing. Sheesh. You're a surly bastard, you know that?"

Clinton rolled his eyes. "I don't care."

Matthew snorted. "Fuck. Jessica deserves better than you."

Clinton's wolf snapped. He rolled to his feet, about to launch himself at the bear, but he held himself back.

Maybe she did. But she was going to get better than him. Because she wasn't his mate. No matter how much his wolf wished she was… no matter how much he wished she was. She wasn't.
And that was never going to change.

CHAPTER FOURTEEN

Trevor sighed as he cuddled a little closer to Jessica, trying to prevent the cold draft that had entered their sleeping bag—or rather, two sleeping bags zipped together—ever since Clinton had left them a few minutes ago. Three months had passed with this uneasy alliance and tensions were getting worse every day. At first, the wolves and Jessica mingled with the other shifters enough, and they'd even had some good times.
But these days? First, there was the tiger, whose lusting eyes seemed to be getting worse the more Jessica's pregnancy showed. Then there was Nikola, who always seemed to have a million things up his sleeves. Lately, it seemed to Trevor that he was probing the cracks in this alliance, testing which one was the weakest and which one he ought to break when the time came.
Jessica could sense his tension and shivered as she lifted her head. "Should we get up?"
"Nah, there's nothing to get up for." He held her tighter, enjoying both the warmth of her form against him and the contented way his wolf stretched out in his chest. He hadn't felt it this lazy in years. Actually, he couldn't remember the last time he'd ever felt it this relaxed. He

buried his face into the crook of Jessica's neck, and she let out a heavy, satisfied sigh.

Clinton absolutely refused to do even kisses, stating that the others in their coalition didn't need to have a peepshow, but Trevor enjoyed the occasional taste of Jessica's creamy skin. There was really nothing like it. It also helped her relax, which could only be a good thing. She was getting close to six or seven months pregnant now and she was getting bigger. Sleeping in a cave day in and out was highly uncomfortable for her, especially since they didn't have the best food for a pregnant woman.

The worst part of the situation was that her clothes no longer fit her. Clinton was able to patch together some makeshift clothing for her since they did bring a sewing kit along, but it meant that her clothes were uncomfortable, ugly, and she didn't have that much.

With other shifters still after them, however, they couldn't just run out and take her shopping. Trevor had had quite a time arguing just to go get her prenatal vitamins. He had picked up some clothes he thought would fit at the time, but her belly had ballooned in ways that surprised them all. Even now, he wondered if they needed to just take her to a checkpoint so she could have proper medical care. The rules of the competition didn't cover this situation.

Neither Nikola nor Clinton argued either way, but the others all were adamant that they were not taking Jessica anywhere and risking losing their prize. If Clinton had backed him up, Trevor would have taken the risk and gotten Jessica to the city and a hospital, but without his partner, there really wasn't anything he could do. He wouldn't be able to outrun them himself and losing Jessica now would only put her in more danger.

So they were staying at the Rockery, first for weeks and then for months. They were starting to talk about moving on, getting to the final checkpoint before they needed to deliver her to the finish line. There the money would be divided up between the others and Clinton and Trevor would go back to Deville empty-handed... at least that was the plan.

Oliver was getting more and more antsy. He kept giving Jessica eyes that made Trevor's wolf want to attack him, and Trevor was convinced that he was planning on double-crossing them. Then of course there were the private conversations Nikola was having with all of them, the increased hunting when it was just Carlos and Matthew...

All in all, it was looking like their coalition was going to fall apart sooner rather than later.

Which was why Trevor did not like leaving Jessica alone, not even for a few minutes. He kissed up her neck to her ear and whispered, "Are you hungry?"

"No," she whispered back. "Actually I feel a little sick. Like if I move I'll puke."

Trevor frowned as he pushed himself to his elbow, smoothing her hair. "That is more than a little sick. Where's your water?"

"Water just makes it worse."

They'd almost run out of rations. He and Clinton had set aside a good portion for Jessica's since their hunting really didn't sit well with her. He had tried to forage for meatless options, but it turned out that his knowledge of which berries and roots were edible was sorely lacking. In any case, Jessica was not doing so great at keeping things down.

"Don't worry," he told her. "Soon we'll be heading back to civilization and we'll finally get you to a doctor. I just hope that they don't count this as mistreatment."

Jessica sighed. "Back to civilization. And then this will all be over."

Trevor flinched as he looked away. That was true. It was all going to be over soon. He didn't really like that. He wished that it could last a little longer. Only without Nikola and the coalition hanging around. Just him and Clinton and Jessica.

"We'll be back in Deville before you know it," he murmured.

She gave him a stiff smile, the type of smile when she didn't want to contradict him in case someone was listening, but she didn't agree with him.

What she didn't know was that he and Clinton had a plan. They had avoided spending any time together when it was just the two of them so that the others wouldn't suspect, but they didn't need words to communicate. They were finally going to get away from these other shifters, and they were going to get Jessica to the finish line and get that money themselves. And from there... well, Trevor had a few ideas of what could happen next, but that really depended on Jessica and what she decided to do.

Even though she was pregnant with someone else's child, Trevor found he didn't really care. He wanted to be with her. If he'd been hesitant at first, the days and months of being here, sleeping with her in his arms, watching her laugh and smile, seeing her get silly, lose her temper, start a yelling match with Oliver and even punch him in the face once... it made his wolf so happy. He couldn't recall ever being as happy as he was when she was right there with him.

Deep in his heart, he knew why that was. He had the words he longed to say. Sometimes his wolf pressed against his chest, nearly making those words pop out, even though he knew that Jessica was in no way ready to hear them.

Even worse was that Clinton was nowhere ready to hear them, either. Even since they had come to the Rockery he had been surly and withdrawn. Trevor could see him wanting to dote on Jessica, could see him holding himself back from showing true emotion around her. It was frustrating, especially since Trevor couldn't exactly ask him what was going on.

Nikola had noticed, and Trevor had told him that it was just a matter of Clinton being a private person. The jaguar had smirked at that, and Trevor didn't like it at all.

Speak of the Devil. Trevor grunted as both Clinton and Nikola came into their little cave space. Jessica groaned as she hid her face from them, and Trevor rested a hand on her shoulder.

"Jessie's not feeling great today," Trevor said.

"Sorry about that, but this should help her feel better," Nikola said.

Jessica lifted her head while Clinton sent Nikola a mild glare. "We're heading out. The closest checkpoint is the Magnus Academy, and it's about time we get you to a doctor."

Jessica pushed herself upright, the sleeping bag falling off her shoulders. "Will I be allowed to sleep in a proper bed or are you going to spirit me away before I get a proper rest again?"

"We want you to have a proper checkup," Clinton said as he knelt on her other side. "That is going to be our top priority."

Trevor tried to keep his expression smooth. If that were the top priority, Clinton would have backed him up and they would have gotten Jessica to a doctor already.

Nikola seemed to catch something in his face, though, because he grinned. He leaned against the doorway and yawned lazily. "Don't you two know the people in the Magnus Academy? Didn't you work with the dragons—"

"No," Clinton spat. His eyes darkened with anger as he turned to Nikola.

Trevor repressed a sigh, wanting to tell him to calm down. He really was taking this too far. Dragons were considered the strongest of all the shifters, but not all of them took that to heart. Not all of them were like the dragon who had taken them as slaves.

"Our pack knows the people there," Trevor said evenly. "Our Alpha, Sly, worked undercover for a while with them. But Clinton and I have only met a couple of the dragons and then only briefly. In any case, if we're going to get moving we had best start. I don't like that Jessica hasn't had a checkup and she's seven months pregnant."

Nikola arched a brow. "Thought it was six."

Jessica pushed the sleeping bag off and got to her feet. "It's somewhere in there, but I don't know for certain. Which is one reason why getting to a doctor would be good. Oh…" She sank back down, looking fairly green. "I don't know if I'll be able to go anywhere today."

Trevor pressed a hand to her forehead, checking her temperature. She felt a little clammy but not too bad. Clinton strode to the back of the cave, where they had their rations hanging up, and retrieved some stale crackers.

"This will help," he told her as he pressed them into her hand.

Jessica sighed. "Renee would have taken me to a doctor already."

Trevor's wolf growled at the mention of the dragon. He bit back the instinctual urge to snap at her that she didn't know that at all, that she couldn't know that because she barely knew Renee. Clinton looked annoyed, and Nikola's eyes gleamed. He didn't mention it, though, and only shrugged.

"It's too bad that you weren't just alone with your mates, then," he said. "Or with Renee."

Jessica cast him a glare but didn't reply. Nikola burst into laughter and sauntered away, waving jauntily over his shoulder in a way that made both Clinton and Trevor glare at him. Trevor would have felt a lot better if the jaguar wasn't so interested in all of their personal business.

"The sooner we get away from them, the better," Clinton muttered. "Back to the pack, with people I can actually trust."

"Do you trust me?" Jessica asked like she didn't really think about it. Then her eyes widened, and she slapped both her hands over her mouth.

Clinton stared at her for a moment and then turned his face away. "Of course I do," he said stiffly. "You're our mate, aren't you?"

Trevor repressed a sigh as his wolf slumped against his ribs. Nobody listening in would think that was anywhere close to the truth. Great. There was so much he wanted to say, so much he wanted to make them see. But he couldn't, not here, not now. There was just too much else happening for him to take the journey right now. To get them to understand that Clinton had just told the truth without even knowing it.

But neither of them was ready to hear that they really were mates. It didn't matter that Jessica was pregnant with someone else's child—even though jealousy burned in Trevor every time he thought of her with someone else—she was their mate.

Now he only needed to get them both to a place where they could understand that.

CHAPTER FIFTEEN

Jessica was pleased that the trip to the Magnus Academy, though long, was uneventful. It took them almost a week to get to the academy, but when she was finally able to have a shower, a proper meal that didn't end up with her feeling sick, and to sleep on an actual mattress, she felt loads better. The head of the Magnus Academy, Maura, was her check-in person this time, and she looked unhappy when Jessica told her that she'd been living in the woods for almost four months.

"They should have brought you here right away," Maura said, shaking her head. "I'll have Dr. Utopia look you over right away."

Jessica nodded. The baby was moving, kicking at her ribs with that rapid-fire movement that they always did at this time of day. She rubbed her stomach, sighing. "It will take a load off my mind. I would like to point out, though, that Trevor argued in favor of getting me doctor supervision but was overruled but Matthew, Carlos and Oliver. Nikola and Clinton didn't say anything one way or the other."

She rubbed her palms over her thighs as a little stab of disappointment hit her. Why hadn't Clinton said they should take her to get a doctor's appointment? If he knew that the baby she carried was either his or Trevor's, would he have changed his mind? Or was he thinking that it would put her in more danger because then other contestants would snatch her from them?

"I'll make a note," Maura said. "And any mistreatment?"

Jessica hesitated then sighed. "Oliver has been creeping me out but hasn't done anything that is strictly against the rules."

"Creeping you out how?"

Jessica folded her hands over her knee. Why couldn't she just keep them still? "Looks, mostly. Comments. To prevent the others from... pursuing me, I agreed with Trevor and Clinton to pretend to be their mate, but that has not exactly deterred him. He has made me uncomfortable with his suggestions multiple times and he only stops when one of the others step in."

Maura frowned. "I'll see what I can do about that. Anything else to report?"

Jessica folded her hands. "I just want to see the doctor right away."

"I understand. We can talk again later."

Jessica breathed a sigh of relief. She was supposed to give a full report, but she didn't want to have to try to muddle her way through everything when she was worried about her baby. Maura took her to see Utopia and she was able to have her checkup quickly. The tests that came back were all good, and Utopia assured her that everything looked like she and the baby were healthy.

During the ultrasound, they got a message that Clinton and Trevor wanted to come in, and Jessica hesitantly allowed it. The image of the baby on the ultrasound screen made Jessica full of warm, fuzzy emotions. For some reason, looking at her baby's face made her want to cry. Trevor laughed and put an arm around her, his expression almost... awed. Clinton looked everywhere except the ultrasound.

Jessica lowered her hands to either side of her stomach,

while Utopia once more assured her that everything looked like it was normal and in order. When she looked back up to thank the doctor, she caught a look at Clinton's face.

He had finally looked at the ultrasound. The hard lines of his face had softened, a soft smile starting to grow on his lips. The tension he always carried in his shoulders faded. Jessica's breath caught in her throat. Her palms pressed more firmly to her belly. She had never seen him looking like that before. So relaxed. So... happy.

And he didn't even know that this baby was his.

They really did deserve to know the truth. She hadn't had the chance to tell them over the past few months. Either she was feeling sick or they would have run the risk of being overheard. But now, here? She could tell them at last. She could finally be honest, finally be open about what was really happening here. She took a deep breath as Utopia took a few pictures of the ultrasound to give to her.

"Can I have a moment with Trevor and Clinton alone?" Jessica asked.

Utopia smiled at her. "Of course. Here's a towel to clean up that jelly. I'll be back in a little bit."

Jessica nodded her thanks. The image of the baby was still on the screen, with Trevor and Clinton both still watching it. Trevor's smile had faded into a strange sort of longing while Clinton had closed off once more. Jessica hesitated as she wiped the jelly off her belly. How did she tell them this, now? What if they thought she was just trying to manipulate them into keeping her? She told them that she wanted a mate out of this, but with the situation that they had created she wasn't going to get one. What if they thought that this was her attempt at getting them to be her mates?

No. It would make things too complicated right now. She had to find the right time, and the right time would be once this competition was done. Then she could call up Renee and at least have the perception of a relationship happening so that the wolves didn't think she was just trying to get them to take care of her.

"What did you want to talk to us about?" Trevor said gently.

Jessica shook her head. "Just that Utopia says that the baby is healthy. So I don't think that anything bad has happened because we were kept at the Rockery. I wanted you to know that."

She glanced at Clinton, trying to say that she wanted him to know it, too, but his face had completely closed off. Her heart sank. Maybe she should have just told the truth from the start. They weren't the kind to let themselves be manipulated, anyway. And it wasn't like she would have started planning out their lives together, anyway! She licked her lips—there was no time like the present.

Before she could speak, though, Clinton broke in. "We don't have much time. Sorry, Jessie, but you are not going to have your mattress here again."

Jessica stared at him. They had taken a day as soon as they arrived just to get the sleep they needed. Due to her pregnancy, they had another full day in the safety of the checkpoint. Her heart sank as she realized that this was going to happen exactly as it had at that first checkpoint. They weren't going to stay here and rest up and plan anew. No. They were going to grab her and run off. Jessica's hands tightened as her baby started moving again. "I don't want to go anywhere. I am tired, I feel sick, I want a proper meal, and I don't want to be stressed out about the others in the coalition finding us and beating the crap out of you for double-crossing them."

Trevor sighed as he put a hand on her shoulder. "I know it's a lot to ask of you right now, Jessica, but this is our only chance. If you want part of the prize money, you'll have to do this, too."

"And don't think that any of the others aren't planning the same thing. Not to mention the other contestants that will be swarming the Academy soon enough, since they'll have learned by now that we've arrived with you." Clinton's gaze was severe. "I know this is hard for you and I know that it's not ideal, but we have to get moving. Think about it this way. You need the prize money to help take care of that baby."

She glowered at him, hating the situation. Beth had been right. This whole competition was a bad idea. Maybe it wouldn't have been so bad if she wasn't pregnant, but she was. And now she had so many things to worry about...

Clinton's frown deepened while she leaned into Trevor's touch. "Of course," he said, his voice brittle and uncertain at the same time, "if you wanted to be with one of the others, we could still work it out so they are part of this. Nikola, if you want."

Jessica snorted. The jaguar was handsome and fun to be around for sure but trying to imagine herself dating him was a big old, 'uh no'. She shook her head. If there was anybody in this coalition that she could see herself trying to have an actual relationship with, it was these two. The ones that she knew she couldn't have a relationship with.

Well. Clinton at least didn't want a relationship. No matter how happy he looked when he was gazing at that ultrasound. No matter how soft and tender his touches were as they lay curled up at night. Trevor was easy, open and always affectionate. Often teasing her, making sure she had what she needed. From the way he stole kisses and whispered sweet nothings in her ear, it was easy for her to forget that they were only playing at a relationship right now.

Clinton, though, remained so closed and stoic. She didn't know what he was thinking.

With a heavy sigh, she shook her head. "I don't want any of them. Oliver gives me the creeps, Nikola is so smooth I never know when he's telling me the truth, and I don't really have any sort of personality understanding of Matthew and Carlos. So. That's that. What's the plan, then?"

"We have half an hour before we're getting out of here,"

Trevor told her quietly. "We just need you to okay your departure with Maura before we leave."

"Fine." Jessica sighed again as she swung her legs off the table. "Let's get this over with then."

As they headed to go talk with Maura, Jessica couldn't help but feel her heart sink lower with every step. She should have known that this place wouldn't offer the shelter that she wanted. Even just one more day would help her get back to some sort of equilibrium. It was awful, really, feeling this way. She didn't want to have this exhaustion and sickness weighing her down.

Even worse was the emotional angst.

When the competition was over, she would have to tell Trevor and Clinton the truth. And then explain why she was lying to them. If their reactions to the ultrasound were any indication, they at least suspected that they were the baby's father but all the same. This was not the sort of situation that she had been hoping for when she entered this competition.

She bit her lower lip hard as she thought about the money that she'd get out of this. It wasn't as good as a full million, but she wasn't going to be able to get away from the competitors and win that money herself. No, the best she could do was this set up where she would get a third of it. That would be enough for her to figure out where to go next, at least.

But as she talked to Maura, explaining that she wanted to leave right away while Trevor and Clinton waited outside, all she could think of was that she was going to have to give up her baby. She couldn't take care of another living creature by herself. Money wasn't the only issue. The prize would dry up and she would have to get another job.

There was more than that, though... money could be earned. But how was she supposed to look after a baby? She had always wanted to be a mother but now as she contemplated being a single mother? She knew she wasn't going to be able to do a proper job of it. She'd mess that kid up, no matter how hard she tried.

"If you're sure," Maura said, and it took a moment for Jessica to remember what it was they were talking about. She forced a smile and nodded. "I'm sure," she said. "This is the best choice. For all of us."

CHAPTER SIXTEEN

Clinton didn't like involving the dragons, not even ones that Sly knew and trusted. However, the situation was getting more slippery and they needed all the help they could get. The most important thing here was to make sure that Jessica was safe and not stressed out too much. Ideally, they'd be allowed to stay at the Magnus Academy in safety or at the very least trade out Jessica for a doll or something, a symbol so she could stay, and they could still continue on with the competition. There was no time to argue for that, though. Nikola was probably already getting the others ready to steal Jessica away with no concern for her condition. They certainly hadn't shown any concern for her during the past few months at the Rockery. There had been times when he considered just grabbing her and taking her into town. But it had been safer for her to just keep her where he could stand guard over her. It was better than if Oliver had ended up taking her away, after all.

Now, since Jessica had reported being uncomfortable with Oliver's behavior and expressed a preference for Trevor and Clinton, they had a little more leeway. Normally, nobody outside of the competition was allowed to help any of the contestants. But now, Maura had worked it so that they were able to get a little dragon intervention.

Jessica smiled at Fiona, a tiger shifter mated to the head of the Blaze Ops, as Fiona handed her a bottle of water. "Thank you."

"This will help you handle that morning sickness of yours," Fiona said. "I hope that this resolves itself the way that you want it to."

Jessica's smile became fixed. "I'm sure it'll turn out for the best."

There was something in her tone that made Clinton want to press for more details, but he didn't speak. He, Trevor, and Jessica were tucked away in the back of a military van. The Blaze Ops, six dragons, filled up the space while Fiona sat closest to them. Clinton hated being in such close proximity to the dragons, but this was the best way for them to be snuck out. The Blaze Ops were experts at this, after all.

Fiona's mate Patrick eyed Clinton and Clinton glared back. His wolf's fur stood on end as he repressed the urge to snap at the dragon. Patrick shook his head and glanced at Trevor instead.

"We're almost to the drop-off zone. Are you ready?"

"Yes," Trevor said firmly. "Thanks for this."

Patrick inclined his head. "The wolf shifters of Devil Mountain helped out my team in ways we didn't know at the time. The least we can do is return the help to Sly's packmates. I hope that you are able to see this through successfully."

Clinton managed to return the well-wishing with a nod but didn't speak. It wasn't long before the van slowed. The dragons hopped out, shielding the wolves and Jessica somewhat. Evan handed Jessica a small device connected to headphones.

"If you strap this around your belly, you'll be able to hear your baby's heartbeat," he told her. "Just in case you end up worried again."

Jessica took it and tucked it into her bag. "Thank you."
Clinton then pulled her away from the dragons. The woods were crisp and clear in a falling dusk. Perfect timing to stay anonymous. Perfect timing for an ambush. Clinton shook his head as he stripped off his clothes and stuffed them into a bundle before he shifted. Trevor helped Jessica onto his back, and she sighed.

"We're going to have to get a saddle," she said.

Clinton's ears flicked back, and he growled. He was not some animal that needed to be saddled and bridled! He knew that Jessica didn't mean it that way, but it was hard not to be annoyed. All the same, he shoved that part down as he headed into the woods, Trevor by his side. They kept a close watch to their surroundings, and there was only a brief moment of uncertainty when they weren't sure that some howling in the distance was a shifter or a regular wolf.

They arrived at their last cache of supplies, locked in a steel chest in a somewhat protected area that they could set up against the weather, only to find Nikola was already there. He had put up a camouflage tarp as a lean-to and had a meal already prepared. He himself was stretched out on top of a sleeping bag, his hands clasped over his stomach with his eyes closed.

Clinton growled as Jessica slid off his back. He shifted to human form and started dressing. "How do you manage to always stay one step ahead of us, Jaguar?"

Nikola opened one lazy eye and stretched as he yawned. He settled back down licking his lips. "I guess I'm just that smart."

Clinton growled and Trevor rolled his eyes. "What are you doing here? I think you've figured out by now that we have no intention of sharing that prize money with you."

"Oh, yes, I have figured that out. And I'm sure you're thinking of taking out my implant right now."

Clinton shrugged. It didn't take a genius to know that, of course, that was where their thoughts were going to go.

His shoulders were tense despite his efforts in loosening them. Jessica held her stomach, looking between the three of them uncertainly.

"Can we just not fight?" she pressed. "A quarter of a million dollars is still enough. I'm tired, I'm hungry, and I don't want to be caught in the middle of this pissing competition."

With another glare at Nikola, Clinton turned to Jessica. He helped her into a camping chair while Trevor retrieved a sleeping bag to tuck in around her. There were no lights except for that of the moon—a crescent, the shape of a thumbnail—and it was difficult to see her expression, but Clinton still got her food. She dug in hungrily. Trevor ate, too, but Clinton refused.

"Afraid that I drugged it?" Nikola taunted. "Now why would I do that? I wouldn't want to put Jessica's baby in danger, after all."

"Shut up before I decide to take out your implant," Clinton snapped as Trevor made noises of agreement.

Nikola smirked as he rolled into a sitting position, the curve of his lips highlighted by a beam of moonlight. "I don't like your hostility, Clinton. You're always so grumpy. I'm starting to think that maybe it's not worth it to try to work with you. Maybe I should just grab Jessica and take her to the finish line myself. Claim her as my mate and get the prize money."

Jessica looked up sharply, her breath catching in her throat. A surge of jealousy rolled through Clinton. His hands clenched as he narrowed his eyes at the jaguar. "Fuck that shit. You don't want *her* as your mate." As soon as he said it, he knew what it would sound like. He flinched as Jessica inhaled sharply. When he turned toward her, she dropped her head. Trevor glared at him and he flinched again. "I didn't mean it that way. I just mean that *he* doesn't seem the type to be interested in getting a mate, let alone a mate pregnant with another man's child."

"What makes you think that?" Nikola arched a brow at

him. "You really have a poor idea of what other people want and feel, Clinton. Jessica is a beautiful, sexy, smart, funny and overall wonderful woman. I signed up for this competition. What makes you think that I'm more interested in the money than I am in the prize?"

Jessica shoveled the food into her mouth like she was too embarrassed to give herself the chance to speak. Clinton's ears went warm and his hands clenched as he glowered at Nikola.

"Just shut up already," he snapped.

"Oh, please!" Nikola jumped to his feet. "You are one of the most stubborn wolves I have ever met. I handed you the reason why I wouldn't want to claim her months ago. You spent all those months pretending to be mates. But you stop here and now? Why? This is ridiculous, don't you agree?" He slapped Trevor's shoulder.

"Hey," Trevor protested through a mouthful of food. "Don't insult my partner."

"Just admit it already. You are mates." Nikola moved behind Jessica and rested his hands lightly on her shoulders. At Clinton's snarl, he withdrew chuckling. Jessica was tense as she sat there, a fork halfway to her mouth. Nikola shook his head as he stepped up close into Clinton's personal space. "There is a reason why none of the others questioned your story. It's obvious to everyone. Your partner has already figured it out. You're in love. You want her forever. So what's holding you back?"

His wolf growled in confusion. Part of it wanted to shove Nikola out of his space but the other part was... was... it couldn't be agreeing with his words! He wasn't any good for Jessica! She deserved someone who actually knew what he was doing when it came to relationships! She deserved... better.

Instead of answering, Clinton drew himself up. He loomed over the jaguar and glared down at him with his full force. "Back the fuck off."

Nikola did, lifting his hands. He snorted and rolled his

eyes, the whites flashing in the moonlight. "Is he always this stubborn?" he asked Trevor.

But Trevor was staring at his plate and said nothing.

"Shut up," Jessica spat suddenly. She glowered up at Trevor. "Whatever our relationship is, it's none of your business. And I know you're just causing trouble. So just shut up. Do you think that if you were to bring me to the finish line and I told them that you threatened me that you'd get your prize money?"

Nikola backed up another step. He laughed, but this time the sound was strained. "You really are a spitfire, aren't you? But tell me, Jessica. Do you really want to stay with them when they won't even admit what they really feel—"

Clinton had had enough. Without waiting for another word, he lunged. His fist planted hard in Nikola's nose, sending the jaguar falling back several feet. Trevor shouted something and Jessica let out a cry. Nikola scrambled back to his feet, shifting as he sprinted away. Clinton let out a roar as he chased the jaguar off. He was sick of Nikola and his coy little comments. Sick of him always sticking his nose in their business, upsetting their plans, being a pain in the ass every fucking minute of the day.

When he was certain the jaguar was gone, Clinton turned back to the camp. He arrived to find Trevor bent near Jessica, his arm around her as she softly cried.

Surprise swept through Clinton. His wolf immediately pushed him to go to her, but his feet rooted to the spot. What was happening? Did she really want Nikola?

"Idiot," Trevor hissed out at him. He lifted his head and his eyes glittered angrily in the moonlight. "You know that he's going to run straight back to the Academy and tell the others where we are. Now we have to get back on the move. Thanks a lot. Jessica really needed to be denied yet another night of sleep."

Guilt rose in Clinton's throat. He opened his mouth, but no denials or apologies seemed appropriate. So while Trevor comforted her as she cried with exhaustion,

Clinton started to pick up camp. There was no telling how much of their supplies Nikola had wrecked to make this meal of his—or what he was really after when he had been taunting Clinton like that.

It doesn't matter, Clinton told himself fiercely. *It's over and done. Now, all we can do is move forward and get that money. Then we can all go our separate ways… and life will be normal again.*

CHAPTER SEVENTEEN

Two more days. One way or another, this was going to be over in two days. Trevor splashed water over his face, his wolf's nose buried in its tail. He was so fucking exhausted that he didn't know if this was worth another two days.

Being so close to victory, though... he could taste it already. A million dollars. Even split three ways, it was an impressive amount. He and Clinton would be able to give something solid and impressive back to the pack that had saved them and then...

What?

Trevor rocked back into his heels as he turned his gaze toward the sky. They were in an unfamiliar forest and had narrowly escaped several attacks by rival hunters already. He and Clinton had had to get the implants out of no less than five people over these last few days, and his body was still battered and bruised from the attacks. One of the fuckers had hit them with blockers. They'd nearly lost that one, except Jessica had swung a frying pan at the man who'd hit them with blockers and distracted him enough for Trevor and Clinton to pin him down and take out his implant.

Shaking his head, Trevor got back to his feet. This was too much stress to be putting Jessica through. They should get her to somewhere safe and then leave her there. Draw the other hunters away from her. She could get herself to the finish line, claim the million dollars, and then split it with them. But Clinton was being a cunt and refused to allow her out of his sight.

Back at their makeshift camp in an abandoned paper mill factory, Jessica was curled up in a nest made of all the sleeping bags, sleeping softly. Her skin was pale and drawn. Clinton, as per usual, sat close to her. He had a heavy branch that could be used as a club nearby. Weapons were strictly forbidden but that didn't stop some of their competitors from using them.

"What are we going to do once we win this thing?" Trevor asked him as he settled down in a position where he could watch for attackers. "We just going to cut ties and throw Jessica away?"

"Letting her go is not the same as throwing her away," Clinton replied, his tone hard. "She has made no indication that she wants us to keep her, and we can't just decide that she's our mate, Trevor. I know that you've gotten attached to the idea of a baby, but it isn't even ours."

"So?" Trevor shook his head, frustration rising. "What does that matter, Clinton? I know that you feel the bond between us. And no, Jessica hasn't made any indication she wants to be ours. But you haven't made any indication you're willing to do anything but throw her away so can you blame her?"

Jessica stirred in her sleep and Clinton got to his feet. He grabbed Trevor's arm and pulled him to one side, far enough away so they wouldn't disturb her. Trevor watched Jessica anxiously. When she settled again, he let out a sigh.

"Sorry," he mumbled. "I guess I'm feeling the stress. I just want to make sure she's okay, Clinton. I want to make sure that her safety comes first."

Clinton rubbed his eyes before his hands dropped, limp at

his sides. "I know. I feel the same was, Trev. It's just... we don't have any right. It's not like we have been... good people. She needs someone who will protect and take care of her. We can hardly take care of ourselves. Where would we be without Lucy? Where would we be without the pack? How are we supposed to give Jessica the support and help that she needs? Not to mention a baby!"

"We'd find a way. We're not useless, Clint." Trevor frowned at his partner, wanting to impress on him how important all this was. "We can't just run away because we're scared."

"I'm not scared. But we're no good for her, Trevor."

Trevor frowned. His wolf cricked its tail in confusion, and he took a step back. "What do you mean by that? We have been looking after her already. We have kept her safe, protected, sheltered. And these are extraordinary circumstances. She trusted us with her fantasies, Clinton. Do you think she tells just anybody that?"

"But that's not enough!" Clinton dug his hands into his hair, a wild look coming to his eyes. "Sheltering and protecting her isn't enough. Yeah, these are extraordinary circumstances. And I know what to do. But I have no fucking clue how to take care of anybody in *ordinary* circumstances. The day to day. I never wanted a mate, and this is why. You know I'm not good with emotions. I shut down and I can't talk through them. Do you really think Jessica deserves that?"

"So we all go to therapy, like William and Jacob!" Trevor's voice started to raise. If he had known that this was what was holding Clinton back then he would have been able to know what to do a lot sooner. "Would it be perfect? Hell no! Nothing is fucking perfect. Do you throw out a person for making mistakes? Are you going to leave me, too, because you don't know how to express your emotions?"

Clinton rolled his eyes and folded his arms.

"Don't pout at me, Clinton," Trevor warned. "I know that this isn't the ideal time—"

"No," Clinton agreed. "It's not. So let's not distract ourselves."

Clinton turned and headed back for Jessica without a word. Trevor stood there, grinding his teeth together. His hands clenched and his wolf howled. He wanted to jump after Clinton and beat some sense into his stupid head. But that wasn't going to do any good. The tension was getting to all of them.

Once this competition was over, then they would be able to talk properly. Maybe they'd yell, he didn't know. But one way or another it would be resolved. And then… well, he would be able to deal with whatever happened then. Right now, Clinton was right. He needed to not let himself get distracted.

That was hard to do when, only a few hours later, Jessica woke with tears running down her face. Trevor's wolf instantly was on alert, pushing him to go to her. He did so at once, wrapping his arms around her. She stiffened but leaned into him all the same. Clinton hovered nearby, his hands clenched into fists. Like he wanted to beat on someone, but there was nobody to beat on.

"What's wrong?" Trevor asked, his voice soft.

"I had a dream," Jessica sobbed. "I was holding my baby."

Trevor blinked several times. Why was she crying over that?

She buried her face into his shoulder. "I don't want to give it up! I want to keep it. I want to be a mother; I don't want to…"

"But why would you have to?" Clinton asked, looking completely floored.

Trevor understood. His arms tightened as he looked up at Clinton, meeting his eye to make sure his partner would know exactly how important these words were. "For the same reason you don't admit that Jessica is our mate."

Jessica's breath caught. She looked up, her eyes wide. Trevor smiled as he brushed her hair behind her ear, but before he could say anything, laughter rang through the factory. Trevor pulled Jessica to her feet and Clinton came to stand before her as three figures emerged from the darkness. Trevor sniffed, but there was no scent—how had they done that. He cursed as he recognized the faces of their previous coalition. Oliver moved to the left while Carlos moved to the right and Matthew strode right for them.

"I knew that was fake," Oliver taunted. His eyes lit on Jessica. "You are going to be mine, little human. I can't wait until you're screaming my name."

Trevor didn't waste time with words. He launched himself forward, howling. He shifted, his clothes bursting into shreds around him. His teeth snapped at Oliver's face. The tiger dodged as Matthew roared. The heavy bear smashed into Trevor's side, sending him spinning away. Carlos had shifted and was on Clinton, snarling and tearing at his forearms. Trevor ducked under another attack as Oliver sprang across the room, landing lightly beside Jessica.

She screamed. Trevor tried to chase after them, but Matthew grabbed his back leg and dragged him back. The heavy weight pinned him down, and Jessica's screams faded as Oliver dashed away with her.

Carlos made a yowling noise and took off after the tiger. Matthew hesitated, and Trevor used his distraction to lunge and bite into his arm. Clinton leapt onto the bear's back. As Matthew snarled and swiped at Clinton, Trevor held on tighter. He felt his teeth click against something buried under that thick hide and he tore into it. Blood spurted in a wide arc, making his heart jump, but he crushed the implant between his teeth.

Matthew roared in pain. Seconds later, Carlos appeared there again. He was bleeding but took one look at what was happening and launched himself at Clinton. He knocked him off Matthew's back and they went rolling. Matthew retreated, limping on his injured leg. Trevor ignored him as he charged into the fray with a howl.

Fur flew, blood spurted, but when it all cleared, Carlos was human, wrapping up his bloody arm while spitting curses out at Trevor and Clinton. The wolves ignored him and Matthew both. They were out of the competition and therefore no longer anything to worry about. But Oliver had Jessica.

The two took off, following after the trail that the tiger had left. Trevor's heart thumped in his chest, growls repeatedly vibrating through his throat. This was not what was supposed to be happening! They weren't supposed to have to chase down this bastard who had Jessica… they had been delayed so long. Oliver must have known that Carlos would go back to help Matthew.

If he got away? If he was able to hide? Two days. It was plenty of time for him to torment Jessica! Trevor's growls increased as they followed the path. But the scent was getting thinner and fainter…

Until it disappeared altogether, under the scent of a black jaguar.

Said black jaguar sat on a rock overlooking them, his tail flicking back and forth. Rage flooded through Trevor, and he leapt at Nikola. He had set this all up. He was a puppet master from the beginning, toying with all of them. Trevor scrambled up the rock, but Nikola leapt lithely to a nearby tree. He let out a laughing yowl, and Trevor jumped at him again.

But the sound of Clinton's bark made him turn. Clinton barked again, sounding urgent. Trevor dashed after him. The scent of blood grew heavy in his nostrils, and Trevor's heart dropped to his toes. But as he passed through a thick brush, he saw Jessica, her arms wrapped tightly around Clinton's neck. He held her just as tightly. Nearby was the tiger, trussed up, unconscious and naked.

Trevor ignored Oliver and rushed to Jessica. He shifted forms and pulled her into his arms. He kissed her again and again, his wolf yipping and howling with delight. Finally, he pulled her into one last kiss, this one deep and long and passionate. Relief washed through his veins as he pressed his forehead against hers. Clinton hadn't released her through all this but now glanced at Oliver with a frown.

"What happened?" he asked.

Jessica shook her head. "I was fighting him so he stopped to tie me up. He said that I was going to belong to him whether I liked it or not." Trevor and Clinton both snarled but stopped when Jessica shivered. She pulled them away from the unconscious tiger before she continued. "Nikola appeared out of nowhere. He knocked Oliver out and then cut out his implant. I asked him why and he said... He said it just seemed like the most amusing option at the time."

Trevor shivered as he held her tighter. He glanced at Oliver but tugged Jessica away from him. They needed to find another safe place now. Let the tiger take care of himself—otherwise, Trevor might just kill him for daring to touch Jessica. As for Nikola... well. He didn't know what the jaguar was up to, but Trevor was grateful to him.

"Come on," he said, gesturing for Clinton to join them. "Let's get out of here."

CHAPTER EIGHTEEN

After such a tumultuous few months and many times of wishing it was over, Jessica found herself dreading the coming day, when Trevor and Clinton would receive their reward, and this would be the end of it all. Now that it was over, she didn't want it to end. They'd checked into the last checkpoint, they were safe from any further attacks, she had the mattress she had been missing for so long. But she'd trade it all for a few more days with Trevor and Clinton.

There was a knock on the door, and she wiped her face, getting rid of the few tears that had leaked, before she answered. Her heart leapt at the sight of Trevor and Clinton standing on the other side. Trevor grinned at her, although it looked a little strained. Clinton, as per usual, had a scowl on his face.

They stepped into the room and Trevor shut the door softly behind them. Before Jessica had a chance to wonder what it was that they wanted, Clinton got right into it.

"Why do you think you have to give up your baby?"

It was the last question that Jessica was expecting, and she floundered for a moment, not knowing how to respond. Trevor took her hand, squeezing gently. The warmth of his touch bolstered her. She straightened her shoulders and bolstered herself.

"I can't take care of a baby. Not on my own. It wouldn't be fair to the baby. I can't put a child through that."

Clinton's brow furrowed. "But... that doesn't make sense. You're strong, determined. Why wouldn't you be able to take care of a baby? You'll have the finances. I know you'd love your child. So what's the problem?"

"The problem is that I'm worthless," Jessica burst out. She didn't want to have this conversation but here she was. "I can't... I can't put a child through life with a worthless mother. What sort of life would that be?"

The scowl faded from Clinton's face as Trevor squeezed her hand all the tighter. "You're not worthless."

"Then why don't you want to keep me?" Jessica's voice broke. She hadn't meant to say that. She hadn't meant to put it on them to give her a sense of self-worth. It wasn't their fault that she had no self-esteem. It wasn't their fault that she was more trouble than she was worth... It wasn't their job to fix her.

Trevor turned her toward her, his gaze intense. "What makes you think we don't want to keep you?"

Jessica opened her mouth and closed it again. What was she supposed to say?

Trevor gazed at her for a long moment before he shook his head. He started undoing the buttons on her blouse and her heart jumped to her throat. His movements were steady, calm. Clinton eyed her exposed flesh with an almost guilty expression on his face.

"What are you doing?" Clinton asked him. "We're supposed to be resolving issues, not—"

"There are too many issues for us to resolve right now," Trevor said, pushing Jessica's shirt off. His hands cupped her breasts, swollen with milk. The warmth of his touch made shivers of pleasure pool through her, zipping straight to her core. "You, Jessica Byrd, *need* therapy. We'll shop around until we find something that works for you, but we are going to find something that works. Understood?"

It wasn't an offer or a request. An order. Jessica nodded, her mind tumbling over itself as Trevor's hands moved to her pants, tugging them down.

"Good," he continued. "Then that is all we will say tonight. There is a lot that we need to talk about and a lot the three of us are going to have to work through. It's not going to magically solve any of our problems. But... we have won you, Jessica. We claimed you as our prize and now you belong to us." He unhooked her bra then cupped her face in her hands. His gaze was so intense that she couldn't deny him. "And we are going to keep you. You and the baby."

The baby. She still hadn't told them the truth. She needed to. But as she opened her mouth to do just that, Clinton growled. He grabbed her and kissed her, his mouth pressing to hers. Heat flooded her body, desire pooling in every inch of her. She gasped as his hands probed against her form, exploring her desperately.

When he pulled back, his forehead touching against hers, she licked her lips, breathless and having completely forgotten what she was going to say.

"We will be gentle," he growled. Again, not a request but an order. "We are going to take this slow because you're pregnant, and I don't know enough about pregnancy to know what is safe and what isn't. After the baby is born and we have had time to get to know each other's signals better, we will start... experimenting. We'll research and talk and start to explore the darker themes, if that is what you want."

Jessica nodded mutely.

He kissed her again. Jessica's blood surged with desire as Trevor finished stripping off her clothing. Exposed before them, she submitted to every hungry touch, every kiss and every word of desire that passed between them. Trevor and Clinton were faster about taking off their own clothes than they had been taking off hers.

Soon, she was laid down on the bed. Clinton's warm, naked body was beneath her, her back against his chest, as she sat with her legs splayed out. His hands were gentle on her body, stroking her skin and hair as Trevor clutched at her thighs, spreading them far enough apart for his tongue to work its wicked ways inside of her.

Heat built in her tightening core. Jessica's hips bucked as she let out a soft cry, the pleasant sensations already starting to make her clit swell. Trevor chuckled into her, and Clinton kissed her temple.

"I'm not good with words," he murmured in her ear. "I'm not good at expressing feelings. I'm not good with people in general."

Jessica moaned as she struggled to listen to Clinton. "But you—oh!" her breath caught in her throat and she grabbed a handful of Trevor's hair to stop him long enough for her to look into Clinton's eyes. "But you are, Clinton. You're the one who said we needed to talk things over when I told you about my fantasy. I don't think you give yourself enough credit."

"Neither of you do," Trevor said. He sat back on his heels and considered them. "Do we need to talk now?"

"No," both Jessica and Clinton said together.

"I'll stop talking," Clinton promised. "Or at least talking about the heavy stuff."

Trevor laughed again as Jessica nodded her promise. He delved back into her, and she was grateful for Clinton's promise. Soon she was crying out so much that she wouldn't have heard him anyway. The pleasure that Trevor evoked in her was amazing, his tongue doing its work and bringing her to a trembling edge.

Without a word, Clinton and Trevor changed places. Only, Trevor kept himself slightly to one side and wrapped her hand around his cock, and Clinton, already hard, pushed himself into her. Neither of them seemed to have much patience as they started moving. Clinton thrust with shallow strokes, getting deeper as he picked up speed.

Trevor kept his hand fisted around Jessica's, moving her hand in time with his jerking hips.

Jessica was suddenly struck by the fact that this wasn't just sex. This was a promise. With each grunt, each thrust and kiss, they were promising her that she belonged to them and they would never throw her away. Her eyes flooded with tears as the truth of it sank in.

They didn't just want her as a warm body to occasionally fuck when nobody else was available. They wanted her. They wanted to share their lives with her. They wanted to get to know her, to learn her quirks. They wanted to invite her into their lives, to see their flaws. To lay themselves open and vulnerable to her. This wasn't just a one-way street. They were asking her to belong to them, to give herself over totally. To become a better person and help them become better people.

Then heat washed through her, fireworks exploding beneath her skin, and she lost her thoughts entirely. The world was limited to this moment, to Clinton thrusting into her, his face contorted with pleasure. Trevor's hisses in her ear as she pumped him, his hand now locked over her wrist. Her core tightened, her thighs clenching. A low throbbing, fluttering filled her and suddenly she clamped down. An explosion swept through her and she screamed in delight while Clinton roared.

Seconds later Trevor had her head in his hands, his cock in her mouth as he spurted. She sucked him down eagerly, trying to keep up with the flow.

Once they were all sated, Jessica lay between her newfound mates, a smile on her face as the relaxation coiled through her body. "You're right. That can be pretty fun, too."

Clinton kissed her shoulder. "It doesn't have to be different or kinky in order to be amazing."

"I do like kinky, though," Jessica said.

"We'll explore," Trevor promised her. "We have a long, long time to figure it all out, after all."

That was true. Jessica smiled happily as a new sort of

warmth swept through her. She couldn't ever recall feeing as safe and happy as she did at this moment. Her fingertips lightly stroked over their skin, her mind flooded with all sorts of delightful thoughts about what they were going to do in the future.

Trevor nuzzled her neck and Clinton kissed her forehead. "I love you," they both whispered in unison as though they had planned it.

"I love you, too," Jessica murmured back.

Then she remembered. This moment wasn't perfect. It couldn't be perfect—because she was still lying to them. Anxiety started to beat at her chest, and she swallowed hard. Doubts crashed in all around her, but she took a deep breath and forced herself to speak before she lost her nerve.

"I lied."

Her wolves looked up, confusion on their brows.

Jessica sucked on her lower lip a moment before she blurted out the truth. "The baby is yours. I didn't tell you, but I was going to tell you. I lied because I didn't... I didn't want you to think I was manipulating you. Or maybe I was sabotaging myself. I don't know. It doesn't make any sense, looking back. But I lied when I said that you weren't the fathers. I... I'm sorry."

Her cheeks warmed and she hung her head, ashamed of herself. Silence passed and she tried hard to tell herself to be patient while her heart thrummed. They deserved the time to process what she had said, and it was a lot for them to wrap their minds around.

Trevor spoke first. "You were planning on telling us... when?"

"Before the baby was born. So that we could make the arrangements for you to take them. Rather than giving them up for adoption."

He nodded, his gaze somewhat distant. Jessica waited. They still stroked her skin softly, but it was driving her crazy that she didn't know what they were thinking.

Minutes passed by before Clinton nodded once.

"Alright. I suppose I suspected that you were lying. My wolf knew. But that's that. We will have to talk about this more," he added with a stern look. "But not right now. I understand why you would lie in those circumstances, and we don't need to worry about it right now."

"Agreed," Trevor said with a nod.

Jessica's eyes flooded with tears. She pressed herself tighter to the both of them, the baby inside of her doing flips now. They were together. The four of them. And that was all that mattered.

CHAPTER NINETEEN

Finally. Clinton grinned as he slipped his arm around Jessica. The rest of the contestants had gathered at the checkpoint and now he, Jessica, and Trevor stood in front of them. A few of their competitors that had been kicked out of the hunt were there, too. The dragon, Renee, grinned when they were announced as the winners. She looked so happy for Jessica that Clinton's normal distrust of dragons cooled.

Their coalition was there, too. Carlos and Matthew looked on with annoyance combined with a begrudging respect, and Nikola smirked as though he had planned it all. Oliver was not there, thank goodness. After the ceremony was done and the check handed over to Clinton—he made sure to immediately deposit it into his bank account via picture—he, Trevor and Jessica went to meet them.

"I'll admit, you did a good job," Matthew said as he held out his hand. "I hope that the three of you have a long, healthy and happy life together."

Clinton found himself smiling. He'd been doing that a lot since the previous night. His hand rested on Jessica's belly—his mate pregnant with his child—and his grin widened. "I'm sure we will."

"I hope you have a good plan for that money," Nikola said, his normal cheerful smile on his face. "I'd hate to have lost out on all of that dough for nothing."

Clinton would have gladly told him to go fuck himself since the jaguar had done nothing but cause trouble—except for saving Jessica from Oliver when they might have been too late—but Jessica answered before he could.

"We do. We're putting it all in the college fund for the pack. We've got a lot of people who want to get more education and a lot of children, too. How many are there now?" She stroked Clinton's hand over her stomach. "With this one it'll be... ten? Eleven?"

"Something like that," Trevor agreed. "And most of those are firstborns, too."

Nikola sighed. "Well fuck me. You've got actual noble intentions. Well, I wish you luck."

He gave a supercilious bow and walked away, shaking his head. Clinton rolled his eyes as he did so. There were a few more people that they were forced to talk to, but Clinton found that he didn't mind it so much. Renee made sure that Jessica knew that she was available if things didn't work out with Trevor and Clinton—causing both wolves to hem her in a little tighter—but soon enough they were on their way back to the hotel.

Once they were in the hotel, Jessica cranked up the AC. When Clinton asked her why she gave him a devilish grin. "I miss snuggling when it's too cold outside to get out of our blankets."

Trevor laughed. With the tension and worries of the past few months fading away, they all climbed into bed. Clinton held his mate tightly, loving everything about her. Her smell, the feel of her warmth against him. There wasn't anywhere he'd rather be than right here. But there was something that he needed to bring up. With everything else going on it had almost slipped his mind, but now that they were well and truly together, he did need to talk about it.

"You said that you didn't want to go back to Deville," he murmured. "Was there a reason for that? Because we can go somewhere else. Move to the city and come back to visit the pack on weekends or something."

Jessica blinked several times, looking surprised. Then, slowly, she smiled and shook her head. "No. No, that's not necessary at all. I was going to leave Deville because I didn't think I could stand to be there… and not with you. We'll figure this out," she promised. "Everything is going to be fine."

Clinton smiled, kissed her, and his wolf snorted in delight. It would have liked to do a little more, but Jessica yawned and so they were both content just to snuggle. Trevor grinned as he pressed his lips to Jessica's temple and the three of them drifted off into sleep.

Clinton woke sometime later to find Nikola sitting on the table next to the door.

"What the—" Clinton jumped out of bed, his lips pulling back in a snarl. He lifted his hands, his wolf surging forward and ready for a fight.

Nikola didn't so much as twitch. His green eyes danced with laughter as he leaned back, a grin spreading over his face. "I was wondering when you'd wake up. You three are so cute. I've never heard synchronized snoring like that before."

Jessica pulled the blankets up to her chin and Trevor put a protective arm around her. Clinton continued to glare at the jaguar. He didn't bother to ask how Nikola had gotten into the hotel. He'd just lie anyway. Clinton took a deep breath, calming his wolf, and asked, "What the fuck are you doing here?"

Okay, maybe he wasn't that calm after all.

The jaguar crossed his legs and took a sip from the glass at this side. "I'm here for my cut, of course. We had an agreement if you recall. I get Jessica, you get the money."

Clinton snarled blackly.

Nikola lifted his hands. "I'm flexible. It's clear to see that you're mates, so I'll be happy with you getting Jessica while I get the money."

"Forget about it and get out," Jessica snapped. "That is *our* money."

"I'm a reasonable man and I'll settle for a quarter of the prize—monetary prize," Nikola added quickly, his grin only getting bigger. "I'm not asking for a piece of Jessica. You are a sexy mama," he winked at Jessica making Clinton scowl, "but I'm not into women who have mates already."

Clinton snorted. He strode forward, and Nikola jumped lithely to his feet. "You're not getting anything from us, Jaguar. We have our prize and you can just leave us alone."

"But a bargain is a bargain."

"We never made any bargains with you." Clinton grabbed Nikola by the back of his neck and hauled him toward the door. "Now get out of here before I lose my temper."

Nikola only laughed as Clinton marched him to the door and threw him out. Once Nikola was gone, Clinton relocked the doors and moved the chair in front of it, to make sure that Nikola couldn't sneak back in. He went back to bed, but Jessica and Trevor were both frowning.

"He can't get back in now," Clinton assured them.

"That's not what I'm worried about," Trevor said. He rolled over and grabbed a laptop. "Nikola has been ahead of us on everything since this started. Do you really think this would be his one exception?"

No. It wouldn't. Clinton frowned as he slid back into bed. Jessica leaned into his side, watching. Trevor's expression was intent on the laptop. Soon, it morphed into frustration and anger. Without a word, he turned the laptop so they could see what was going on. And there it was, in all its glory. First, the transfer of the million dollars into Clinton and Trevor's joint account. Then, right after it, a transfer of $250,000 *out* of the account.

"He's already got it," Jessica murmured. "That bastard."

Clinton fought down the urge to go after Nikola and beat

the crap out of him. He was probably long gone by this time. He shook his head. "Well, he did take care of Oliver for us."

"Yeah," Trevor agreed. "And he could have taken more."

Jessica snorted and shook her head. "So we're just going to let him have it?"

"Of course not," Clinton replied. "But let's look at this logically. Do you think it's going to be possible to get it back?"

Jessica slumped back. "No. Not when it comes to him. Ugh. But... but I guess it's still a lot of money, anyway. I just hope that he has noble intentions with that. Like he's got a sick mother and he needs to pay for her medical bills. Something like that. Not that I would really wish sickness on anyone..."

She let out a sigh and shook her head. Clinton kissed her, laughing. Normally he would be the furious one, but there was just something about the situation that made it impossible for him to be all that angry. There were just too many good things that had happened in the last few days.

"It's fine. Money is an easy way to contribute to the pack. With how rich Theron is, it's not like we really need the money." Clinton settled back, an arm around her shoulders. "We'll figure something else out. In the meantime, let's just be with each other here. Because we have our whole future to figure out, and it's going to be one hell of a ride."

EPILOGUE

"I get to hold the baby first," Lucy declared as soon as Clinton, Trevor and Jessica arrived at her place to celebrate her new job... and to be sad that she would be moving away from Deville, at least temporarily. Lucy gently took baby June out of the car seat and cooed at her while Clinton put an arm around Jessica's waist and Trevor carried the potato salad over to the buffet table.

"Sorry we're late," Jessica said, noting with embarrassment that everyone else was here already. "We took a nap and someone," she sent a mild glare at Clinton, "unplugged the alarm clock."

Lucy laughed and shook her head. "It's fine. The kids are getting hungry, though, so we better start eating."

Jessica smiled as she glanced around the pack. Mothers and fathers rounded up their children, herding them toward the food so they could start eating. Everybody talked and laughed with each other and a sense of warmth burned in Jessica's chest as she hung back, Clinton staying with her and Trevor quickly returning to them.

Now that she was here, with her mates, her baby, a pack and friends she could rely on, she couldn't fathom how she had ever survived before. She couldn't think of how she would have survived leaving Deville. This place had become home. She couldn't bear to even think about leaving it. As her gaze lingered on Lucy and baby June, her heart gave a twinge.

"It's not going to be the same around here without you," she told her friend.

Lucy glanced up and nodded. "I know. It's all very strange and quite intimidating. I never thought that I'd leave my boys. But this job opportunity is for the best. I can't stand working for Bill anymore... He's going to lose his business, the way he keeps working the girls he hires. But, we're not here to talk about him." A smile spread over her face as she adjusted June. "How are you guys doing?"

"It's been tiring," Trevor laughed. "But good."

Jessica nodded her agreement. Life was amazing. She was filled with hope and excitement that she never thought she would have. Her dreams were coming true, and it made waking up in the morning an adventure.

That didn't mean that everything was perfect. She didn't magically have amazing self-esteem and she, Trevor, and Clinton didn't magically know exactly how to communicate perfectly. There had been ups and downs, but the important thing was that they were all trying, and they were all making the effort to figure out what they needed to do to make this work.

The baby meant they had to work that much harder, but every second was worth it.

And she still had moments of serious doubt about whether or not she could be a mother, but the girls in the book club had banded together to find her a therapist. It was still in the early stages, but there were already tricks that she'd learned to help negate the worst of it if she caught her spiraling thoughts soon enough. They were talking about medication, too, but Jessica wanted to give therapy an honest try first.

Beth, William, Jacob, and Tanya came over with their

plates full of food. Tanya bounced all around Lucy, trying to get June's attention until Clinton knelt beside her and asked her how school was going.

"Great!" she shouted, bouncing some more. "I got 100 on my test and the teacher read my story to the class! Next week we are taking a field trip to see the dinosaurs!"

"That is amazing," Clinton said enthusiastically.

Tanya nodded. "Yeah, and Mama Beth is gonna have a baby, and I'm gonna be a big sister!"

Jessica turned surprised eyes onto Beth, who flushed vividly. Jacob laughed and shook his head while William shushed Tanya. Jessica hugged Beth, congratulating her, and Beth told her to go get some food before it was all gone. Lucy nodded at her as well, and so Jessica made her way to the table. Angela with her mates Max and Tyler were picking out food suitable for their little twins and nodded to Jessica in agreement.

"I take it Tanya told you that Beth is pregnant?" Angela asked with a twinkle in her eye.

"She did," Jessica replied. "She's very excited."

"She's been talking about it non-stop," Angela said with a roll of her eyes "I would say she is excited."

Jessica chuckled. "How's the farm doing?"

"Good. We got a good harvest from the sheep's wool this year. I've been cleaning and carding non-stop. Well…" She looked at the twins with their fathers. "I should say between looking after those little munchkins. They're getting into everything. They grow up so fast."

Jessica nodded. It'd only been a few weeks since June was born, and she had already seen major changes in her. "I know what you mean. Time goes quickly. Especially when you're sleeping all the time."

Angela put a gentle hand on her shoulder. "It'll pass. You will get back to a sense of normalcy before too long."

"It'll be a new normal, though," a voice behind her said. Jessica turned to see Jamie with her mates, Adrian and Shawn. The men nodded at her as they collected their food, with Adrian getting enough for Jamie as well. She rubbed her stomach, which was swollen with pregnancy. "Things will never go back to the way they were."

"I don't want them to," Jessica said fervently.

"Speaking of..." Jamie gave Angela a sly grin. "I heard that the Paranormal Surrogate Agency contacted you, asking if you wanted to be a surrogate again."

"They did," Angela said, stepping to one side to allow Miriam's nephews access for their second helpings. "You'd think that after this long and the way they messed up things to start with they wouldn't bother. I told them no, of course. Max and Tyler want more kids and so we're trying ourselves. We don't want to put it off, even though the money was good."

Miriam joined them. "I just wish more people would think of adoption. But I guess adoption can be even more expensive."

"You can adopt," Jessica suggested.

"We're talking about it. We have three boys already, though," Miriam said with a slight shake of her head. "I don't want to end up not giving them the time they need."

"I understand that," Jessica murmured. "Clinton, Trevor, and I haven't really talked about how many children we want yet, but we are taking our time."

One of the twins called out to Angela so she excused herself. Miriam's mates, Kristoff and Lucas, came over to help the boys, and Jessica took the opportunity to dish herself up some warm steak salad. She'd never had such a thing before, and it sounded interesting. After she filled her plate, she returned to Clinton and Trevor to find Wanda, Omar and Roman had joined them. Omar held June, cooing over her while Wanda rocked their little boy, who had been born just a few weeks before June.

"I'm just saying," Wanda said, sounding exasperated while Roman grinned at her, "it wouldn't kill you to eat more vegetables."

"We're wolves, my love," Roman said. "We don't need

vegetables."

Wanda rolled her eyes.

Jessica ate the delicious food, glancing around at the pack. Ian, Theron, and Sandra stood near Chloe, Devon, and Sly, talking and laughing. Theron had been so impressed by Clinton and Trevor's determination to get money for the children's college funds that he had gone ahead and started a fund for each of the children in the pack. Everyone was able to put in as much as they liked to whatever fund they wished.

Brian, who was foster son to Chloe and her mates, would be starting school in the fall. His intentions were to become a lawyer, specializing in defending shifters against unlawful charges. Everyone was proud of him and he often said that he could never have gotten this far without Sly, Devon, and Chloe.

As she considered the pack, she realized that none of them had thought that they would get to this place in their lives. Whether they thought they were unlovable, unworthy, or didn't have an interest in domestic life until they met their mate, nobody in the pack had started out with this goal. It was a dream for many of them, a dream that had seemed impossible but came true all the same.

Just as it had for her. And as she looked at her beautiful baby girl and then at her wonderful mates, her heart swelled with happiness until she thought it might burst. This was what life was supposed to be. This was why hanging on through the dark times was worth it. Because the sunlight after the storm was all the brighter and warmer for having known what cold was.

"What are you grinning about?" Trevor asked her, sliding an arm around her waist.

Jessica only smiled wider. "I'm just happy. I'm the one who won that competition. And nobody can take my prize from me."

*****

HUNTED BY THE WOLVES

THE END

THANK YOU

Thank you so much for reading "Hunted by the Wolves"!

Hopefully, you enjoyed reading my book as much as I did writing.

I would appreciate if you'd be willing to share a review that allows me to continuously improve my books and motivates me to keep writing.

Also a big thank you to my husband and my son. Your support means the world to me!

P.S. Stay tuned, there are more books in the "Devil Mountain Wolf Shifters" series to follow:

Kidnapped by the Wolves (Book 1)
Sold to the Wolves (Book 2)
Surrogate to the Wolves (Book 3)
Enslaved by the Wolves (Book 4)
Seduced by the Wolves (Book 5)
Promised to the Wolves (Book 6)
Bitten by the Wolves (Book 7)
Hunted by the Wolves (Book 8)

ABOUT THE AUTHOR

Jasmine Wylder is a Real Estate Agent by day and an emerging Paranormal Romance Author & Adventurer by night. Hailing from California, her passion for sultry stories, steamy scenes, and all-things romance began early on and it has stayed with her ever since.

When she isn't creating captivating storylines, Jasmine loves spending time in the great outdoors, practicing yoga, and treating herself to fine cuisine.

Whether it's out-of-this-world love (literally), dragon shifters setting your heart ablaze, or unquenchable vampiric desire, Jasmine has you covered!

Want more of Jasmine Wylder? Stay social with her:

Join her Reader's Group on Facebook:
http://bit.ly/JWylder

Like her publisher's Facebook Fan Page:
https://www.facebook.com/PurePassionReads/

Follow her on BookBub:
https://www.bookbub.com/profile/jasmine-wylder

Follow her on Amazon:
http://author.to/JasmineWylder

Printed in Great Britain
by Amazon